ADVANCE P
GALLERY OF THE D

T0023089

"The stories in Jonathan Papernick's ambitious collection *Gallery of the Disappeared Men*, all ask a profound question: how do we begin to face our own trauma? Part mythical, part magical, always historical, and forever haunting, this book examines the violence and brutality of antisemitism, racism, and misogyny through a difficult lens; prepare to be shaken by it. I won't forget it."
—Carolyn Ferrell, author of *Don't Erase Me* and *Dear Miss Metropolitan*; anthologized in *Best American Short Stories 2018* and *The Best American Short Stories of the Century*

"Papernick's stories are at turns gritty, heart-wrenching, and quick-witted, but always unforgettable. I'm so excited to know this collection will finally be out in the world. Everyone should read it."
—Sara Nović, *New York Times* best-selling author of *True Biz*

"With his new collection, *Gallery of the Disappeared Men*, Jonathan Papernick once again proves himself a consummate storyteller. From a stark displaced persons' camp to the staid Boston suburbs, to the purportedly cushy camp hills of Orange County, Papernick boldly immerses us in unsettling and disturbing landscapes. Violence is everywhere and often unrelenting, perpetrated by an extensive cast of bullies. But there is magic in the horror too. Children grow gills. A dead mother spams her son. A severed hand morphs into a man. These are brutal stories of a troubled world excavated with surgical precision in a tireless search of the reckless and ruined, ever-beating, human heart."
—Sara Lippmann, author of *Doll Palace, Jerks,* and *Lech*

"As a novelist, Jonathan Papernick is a master at salvaging dignity from human disappointment. He is a fixer in fiction, a storyteller of hidden silver linings, the kind of lively, engaging writer who will make you laugh and squirm and root for a happier ending for his characters—all misfits, outcasts, survivors--many of whom are too cynical or broken to believe in the writer who conjured them. *Gallery of the Disappeared Men* is a master class in Papernick's special talents."
—Thane Rosenbaum, author of *How Sweet It Is!, The Golems of Gotham,* and *Second Hand Smoke*

"I could rave on for hours about how deeply moved I was by this collection. I am awed by how well Papernick writes the perspectives of women, how he writes loss, and how he incorporates Jewish history and the rich pain of our people that remains a shadow of unshakable darkness that lives inside of us. *Gallery of the Disappeared Men* is unique and powerful. And it offers hope, too, by showing how transformative love can be in all its many broken forms of rescue. Each story in this collection is a beautifully crafted ballad, and each character a cantor, who illuminates the deepest forms of loss and offers a survivors' breed of hope, making this a perfect collection for our times."
—Melissa Falcon Field, author of *What Burns Away*

"Prepare yourself. *Gallery of the Disappeared Men* is not a book you can dip into. These stories are transgressive and unafraid. This is a book that will trap you and sentence by sentence bind you more tightly to the fates of characters faced with impossible choices, characters driven by desires they do not understand, characters who search for what seems real. Here are dreams, some of them nightmares, from which you will not easily wake, and which will stay with you long after you do."
—Richard Hoffman, author of *Interference & Other Stories*

"*Gallery of the Disappeared Men* is a knockout collection of stories that promises to both shock and move you. With bright, evocative prose, Papernick dares to shine a light on the disturbing edges of the human psyche, while never losing sight of the goodness often found at the center. In these stories, better selves battle crueler instincts, painful pasts clash with hopeful futures, magical realism dances with harsh verisimilitude, and cruelty and violence occur—as they do in the real world—beside sparks of kindness and conscience. Reader, prepare to sometimes squirm with discomfort, sometimes root with joy, and to never ever be bored."
—Jessamyn Hope, author of *Safekeeping*

"Jon Papernick is a magician, conjuring a rich emotional landscape from his deeply observed characters and their very human lives and needs."
—Ben Tanzer, author of *Upstate, Orphans,* and *Lost in Space*

"Jonathan Papernick's *Gallery of the Disappeared Men* is vicious and truthful, fantastical yet down-to-earth. Each story offers a different angle into the troubled heart of humanity with a keen eye for every palpitation and irregular beat. An equal mix of survivors, victims, and those who fall between such distinctions appear throughout these stories. All of them will linger and lurk in your mind for a long while. Disappear with these men (and women) and find yourself somewhere else indeed."
—Charles Pieper, writer and director of *Malacostraca*, writer of *Destroy all Neighbors* and producer of *Everybody Goes to the Hospital*

GALLERY OF THE DISAPPEARED MEN

Stories

Jonathan Papernick

Gramarye

This is a work of fiction. Names, characters, places, and incidents either are the product of the author's imagination or are used fictitiously. Any resemblance to actual events, locales, organizations, or persons living or dead, is entirely coincidental and beyond the intent of either the author or the publisher.

Gramarye Media
1270 Caroline Street
Suite D120-381
Atlanta, GA 30307

Copyright © 2023 by Jonathan Papernick

Some of these stories were originally published in the following:

"When the Rains Came" *Failbetter*; "Gallery of the Disappeared Men" *Martian Lit*; "The Price of Admission" *Post Road* Magazine; "Adam Number Three" *Folio*; "Saudade" *Frontier Psychiatrist*; "The Cinq à Sept Girl" *ELQ: The Literary Quarterly*; "Emails from My Dead Mother" *Blunderbuss Magazine*; "Dog Whistle" and "Fuck Almighty" *People Holding*; "In Flagrante Delicto" *Blunderbuss Magazine*

The Library of Congress Cataloguing-in-Publication Data is available upon request.

Gramarye Media paperback ISBN-13: 978-1-61188-354-1
Fiction Studio Books E-book ISBN: 978-1-945839-75-7

Visit our website at www.GramaryeMedia.com

All rights reserved, which includes the right to reproduce this book or portions thereof in any form whatsoever except as provided by U.S. Copyright Law. For information, address Gramarye Media.

First Gramarye Printing: April 2023
Printed in the United States of America
0 9 8 7 6 5 4 3 2 1

Also by Jonathan Papernick

I Am My Beloveds
The Book of Stone
There Is No Other
Who by Fire, Who by Blood
The Ascent of Eli Israel

For Those Who Are Gone

CONTENTS

DISPLACED PERSON

I was born twice, once from my mother's womb in the Galician city of Tarnów, and once in the arms of a handsome watchmaker. Enough has been written about the black years of the war when everything I knew was turned upside down; my nightmares are no more and no less vivid than anyone else who suffered, so I will only say that I survived the catastrophe and leave it at that.

After liberation, I was living, if you can call it living—I breathed, and slept, my bones brittle, my legs swollen from starvation—at the Zeilsheim Displaced Persons' Camp in the American Zone, just a dozen miles west of Frankfurt. In the early days I suffered terribly of dysentery and saw in my mind, my mother, my father, my brother and sisters marching before my feverish eyes, forever marching, their arms gesturing for me to join them. I was so tired, and while I wanted nothing more than to feel my mother's warm hand on my forehead, to smell the sweet wood smoke in my father's beard, I knew I did not have the strength, and before long they were swallowed up forever in the darkness. When my fever broke and the stubborn strand of memory connecting me to my family had snapped, I found myself orphaned in the world with the promise of Palestine in my heart. But with the British government being what it was at the time, I felt I would be stranded forever in Germany. It was the cruelest joke one could imagine. Living in the empty homes of workers from the nearby IG Farben plant, I could still hear their voices like ghosts in the walls, rising from the floorboards, proud talk of the important role they played in carrying out the Final Solution.

The crowding was terrible. We were mostly young, there were no children and few over forty years of age. We were all survivors and had all learned to adapt. Before long, a jazz orchestra had sprung up, a theater group, a yeshiva, two Yiddish newspapers, and a mens' sports club named "Hasmonai." Each of the buildings in our temporary haven were named after towns and settlements in Palestine. I lived in an apartment house called Zihkron Ya'akov, and my heart ached knowing I may never escape my cramped flat for a sunny land that flowed with milk and honey.

I passed my time occupied with simple tailoring work such as the residents of Zeilsheim required, believing a trade would guarantee for me a future in Palestine. But my work was solitary, and I kept to myself. Sometimes the pants and shirts and pincushions before me would disappear and I would wake hours later wandering in a field not knowing how I had arrived there, sensing I had sought some impossible reunion.

So many of the other girls were getting married and even having babies, trying to raise a family as fast as possible to make up for their families that died during the war. But I had not had my cycle in many years and knew I was no longer able to bear children, so I remained alone. After more than a year at Zeilsheim I was still afraid to look at myself in the mirror, still in the grips of the skeleton I had seen at the camp, the skeleton with the deep eyes with no bottoms.

"Don't you recognize me?" the face had asked when I saw a reflection of myself in a rain puddle. I could not tell whether I was of the living or the dead.

An American girl from the Joint Distribution Committee named Betty taught me English in the afternoons. She was healthy, not quite fat, from some far-off place in the middle of a vast, impossible continent, far from the sea and the problems of the world. The other girls did not like her. She did not speak Yiddish or Hebrew and knew nothing of Palestine. They said she was not Jewish and had pink skin like a pig's. They complained she could not understand our culture and the ways of our lost civilization. But I knew they only wanted to recount again and again in gruesome detail what had happened in the camps. Their preoccupation with the atrocities we all suffered only caused me to suffer again, as if for the first time. I was happy to have Betty to myself. She smiled easily, like a child who knew nothing beyond her own nursery, and we read simple books together. In turn I read to her from the newspaper *In Transit* and studied the list of missing persons in the hope of seeing a familiar name.

I loved languages and spoke Polish, Russian, German, Yiddish, Hebrew and even a little French, but I could not understand why "enough" did not have the letter *f* or why "though" and "dough" ended in *gh* while "throw" and "so" did not. Or why "sew" did not rhyme with '"stew." I enjoyed the challenge, and Betty was very kind to me.

The doctors told me I had gained back much of the weight I lost, and I wore a new donated, flower-print dress sent from from America. Betty had brushed my hair and fastened it at the back with a pretty, red bow. I felt like some sort of plaything, a child's doll, and I pulled away from Betty and said, testing my English "Why do you doing this?"

"I'm trying to help you get your self-respect back, as a human being, and as a woman."

"Why?" I said understanding little of what she said. I knew she was trying to help me but could not understand why anyone would want to do so.

I was used to being sprayed for lice with DDT, poked with needles to test for tuberculosis. I was used to countless humiliations at the hands of others, but now Betty placed a red leather box between us that lit up when opened and removed a tube of lipstick. I was still as she applied it to my lips, and it felt like I was being kissed. I was reminded that those desires I thought had gone forever still lay in my secret places.

"You're blushing," she said. "Let me help you."

She tickled my cheeks with a soft brush and said, "My mother used to pinch herself to gain a rosy glow. I've always preferred Revlon."

When Betty was finished with my lips and cheeks, applying makeup to my eyes, and plucking the hair on my brows, she took a step back and smiled, her big white teeth shining like the pearls around her neck. She even painted my brittle fingernails a cheerful red, covering over the ugly white spots and splitting the doctors told me came from years of calcium deficiency.

"You look pretty," she said. "Here, I want you to have this." She unclasped her pearl necklace and fastened it around my neck. I was so surprised at first, I did not notice she was showing me my new face in the mirror.

The face of the person who stared back was not me. "Who is that?" I screamed. "Who is that?" I had such a fright I pushed away the mirror. I could not understand where I had gone. This had to be some sort of joke. Where had I gone?

Betty soothed me and caressed my hair like I was a frightened child.

"It's all right, Fannie. It's all right. It's just makeup."

In time, she convinced me to unclose my eyes and look in the mirror again. I did, and I understood part of me had withered away and died. I touched my face with trembling fingers, the high cheekbones, the narrow arch of my brows, the cherry-red lips.

"You look pretty," I said, staring deeply into the mirror.

"Fannie, say '*I* look pretty,'" Betty said.

"I look pretty."

She reached out her hand to me. "The sun is shining. Let's go for a walk."

Out in the street, the men from the Hasmonai sports club were playing a game with a ball and a wooden club. They all wore short pants and matching shirts with Stars of David on their breasts. A tall American with brown wavy hair and a smart, narrow mustache stood at the center of the square and threw the ball at the man with a stick who swung at it and missed.

"Even Teddy Ballgame strikes out once in a while," he said.

His voice was warm and confident and friendly. His eyes were very blue.

"Who is that?" I asked Betty.

"I don't know. He just arrived on Monday. But the other girls call him Kilroy."

I saw him notice me and he stopped for a moment, letting the ball slip from his hands, studying me as the men around him shouted for him to pick up the ball. He bent over without once removing his gaze, then winked at me and tossed the ball to the man with the club.

I told her I would like to watch the game, and Betty smiled. Kilroy moved with ease and grace, stalking like a wolf as he snatched up the ball, throwing it with impressive accuracy to the men standing on empty bags of flour that had been folded into quarters to mark crude stations the men who hit the ball were required to pass. Most of the men caught the ball with their bare hands, but a few, including Kilroy wore padded leather mitts on one of their hands. I was impressed by his ingenuity to invent such a game, but soon I could stand still no longer, and my restless feet carried me away from the cries and shouts of the game.

Betty asked me why I had walked away, and I began to cry, not knowing why the tears had come.

"I don't know," I said in English. And then I began to laugh, because I knew there was "no," and "know" and I was not sure she could understand which I was trying to use.

I was laughing and crying when he approached and handed me his handkerchief. It was warm from his pocket and smelled fresh like laundry soap.

"I'm Laszlo," he said.

"I'm crying," I said.

In the evening Laszlo came to me and asked if I would like to see a concert. The jazz quartet was playing. I had seen handbills for them posted around the camp. I said yes. He was polite, unlike so many of the Americans I had met who were crude, and loud, and talked quickly. I did not wear my new pearl necklace because it was too valuable and hid it away beneath my mattress.

He spoke some Yiddish he had learned from his father, some stilted biblical Hebrew, and of course, English. I was afraid at first to speak, believing he would realize we could not understand each other and leave. Betty had offered to chaperone our "date," but I did not want to share this man who looked at me as if I was something rare. I wanted to ask him what he was staring at, and I was afraid for a moment he saw before him the same wretch I had been. He was so handsome, with impossibly blue eyes and a straight nose above his narrow, trimmed mustache. He took my hand in his and we began to walk. It may seem strange to say that I was not nervous with this man who I had just met, but I felt safe in a way I had not felt since my earliest memories. I felt the warm blood moving through his veins and how its pulsing came to match mine. His hands were so large my hand was lost in his. We walked toward the field where the stars shimmered above. He pointed to the sky and said, "Make a wish, Fannie."

I did not understand what he meant at first; wishes were superstitions like religion, a belief the Messiah would come and save us. But I saw the playful smile on his face, and I laughed. "I wish I was princess."

"You need to be serious," Laszlo said. "Do not tell. Now close your eyes and wish."

He covered my eyes with his soft hands, and I said, "Why?"

"Because I want to make your wish come true."

He kissed me softly on the mouth and I began to cry. "You are making joke on me. I am a *shmatte* with no use."

Laszlo looked surprised—his blue eyes open wide. "How can you think that? You are beautiful." Then, he kissed me softly again and whispered, "You are beautiful."

I could hear the jazz quartet faintly floating on the breeze, a trumpet sobbing. I was amazed by what I was doing; I had never been so daring, but my parents were gone, my family was gone, and I did not have to worry about what they thought. I lifted my dress over my head and lay down. Crickets chirped quietly in the warm grass. Without a word Laszlo lay beside me, removed a silver pocket watch from his jacket and checked the time. He later told me he did that so he could remember the exact moment when our bodies met.

When we had finished, I held onto him, my arms thrown about him with all my strength. My body no longer existed only to experience pain, but also joy. I felt I had been given permission to live, not as the girl my parents had raised in Tarnów, but as the woman I would become.

We walked back, hand in hand, Laszlo kissing my ears tenderly.

"We missed the concert," he said, laughing. "Sing for me."

I sang the only song that came to my mind, the only song for which I knew all the words, a song that brought me comfort at the camps when comfort was impossible. I slowly sang the words of "El Maleh Rachamim," and I felt transported to somewhere above where we stood, floating, and looked down upon the two of us: it was the first time I realized I was still young, and Laszlo was the answer to my wishes. His eyes were full of tears. He did not know the song and when he asked its name, I did not tell him I was singing from habit for the souls of the dead. I simply kissed him.

I did not see Laszlo the next day, or the day after, and began to worry he had left me behind. I fell into a black mood. I did not believe he was capable of doing such a thing, but I worried still. I asked people at Zeilsheim if they knew who Laszlo was and where he had gone, but no one knew. On the third day, a girl who lived across the street in the Herzliya house told me her new husband was a lathe worker in the metal shop at Lampertheim and had met Laszlo when he arrived. He was an American watchmaker who had performed top-secret work on weapons systems during the war and had been brought over by the United Nations to help set up basic machine shops in the DP camps throughout the American Zone. He made inspections, signing "Kilroy Was Here," on each machine when it passed, and when it did not, he added it to a long list of materials the camps needed. He traveled to German factories and installations no longer in use since the end of the war and brought back bits of machinery, spare parts, anything that could be used to help make the camps self-sustaining. He was expected back at the end of the week with spindles and belts and motors.

Betty came to me on Friday morning very excited and told me my cousin had arrived in search of me. I dropped the pants I was hemming in shock that such a thing could happen. I had last seen my little cousins Yossi and Ruchel at Targowica Square before they were deported to the Belzec extermination camp. They could not have survived. I had other cousins, distant cousins from as far away as Sendzishov. I had not seen their names in any of the missing persons lists and thought they had been killed. It was not easy to imagine someone resurrected, as my distant cousins would have to have been if one of them was searching for me now. In a selfish way, I was not happy to hear this news. I was preparing to turn away from the madness of Christian Europe which had been for the Jews little more than slaughters and massacres for the past two thousand years. I did not want to be reminded of what had been lost every time I looked into my cousin's face. I had sworn to never look back again at that dead world. There was simply too much blood and pain and sadness. But my cousin was alive and on his way to see me. It had been so long, and I wondered whether I would recognize him. I had three or four male cousins who were nearly the same age as I was but could only think of one of their names, and Yitzchok had been feeble-minded and surely had not survived.

There was a knock at my door, and I opened it, not expecting to see Laszlo standing in front of me. I had not brushed my hair and I wore no makeup. But he was kind and said nothing about my appearance. Laszlo was dressed in travel clothes and wore a handsome gray hat on his head. He was out of breath and spoke rapidly.

"Fannie, I want you to come to America."

I thought America was not a possibility for me. I had shaken the hand of the widow Roosevelt when she had visited Zeilsheim, and even then, I never thought that I could live in America. I had no relations there, no employment possibilities. My English was not good. It was a dream I had dared not dream. Palestine was the Promised Land and I had imagined many times living safely among Jews in my own country. But the King David Hotel in Jerusalem had just been bombed by Jewish terrorists and many people had died. I was afraid violence would follow me wherever I went.

In the spring when Ilya Kalman and some others had registered with the Joint Distribution Committee to emigrate to America, they had been called traitors by the labor Zionist group. Men had thrown stones at them as they were escorted out of the camp to begin their journey to the USA.

America was the Golden Land, and now I would have the chance to go. I did not care if people called me a traitor.

"I told the relief workers from the Joint you are my third cousin, and I've sworn once you are in the US, you will not be a financial burden. I want to take care of you."

"You want me to live with you?" I said.

"Yes, yes."

I stared at Laszlo with no words. We barely knew each other and he wanted me to travel a half a world away to be with him. He smiled nervously, and I saw in his smile he meant what he said. I thought of our night together in the grass beneath the stars when we behaved as husband and wife and permitted myself to imagine an entire lifetime with this man.

"You need to gain medical clearance to assure you are healthy and free of communicable disease, and then I need to petition on your behalf."

He stood in the doorway expectantly, and I realized he was waiting for an answer.

"I will live with you," I said.

Laszlo picked me up in his arms and swung me around, and for a moment I was sure I was flying. He was so strong.

"I'm leaving now for Munich. I'm flying home tomorrow and will get started right away petitioning for your emigration to Boston."

"What is Boston?"

Laszlo laughed. "It's where the Red Sox come from."

The color of socks mattered little to me, but I was grateful for the chance to be traveling far from Zeilsheim to this new place to be with Laszlo.

He reached into his jacket pocket and removed a silver watch. "This is an American-made, twenty-three jewel, open-face, size eighteen, stem-winder—the most accurate timepiece in the world with less than thirty seconds variation per week. I want you to keep this with you always, until we meet again."

He pressed the watch to my breast, kissed me softly on the lips, and left for America.

A NEW WORLD

I came to Laszlo empty-handed in shabby clothes that were not my own. It had been twelve days since I had boarded the freighter *Amelia* in Liverpool bound for New Bedford, and the donated dress I had been saving to wear when I met Laszlo again no longer smelled fresh. It was wrinkled from my trunk and had fallen into some bilge water after I had hung it up to give it air. I had been saving that dress for so long I wore it anyway. Our reunion was awkward; he had become shy and did not know how to greet me. Laszlo had shaved his mustache and he looked very young. He wore his handsome gray hat and fidgeted with the hatband as if he had misplaced something there. I was afraid he thought he had made a mistake in sponsoring my immigration and stood silently before his inspection, feeling naked.

I had taken care of his pocket watch like it was my own child, winding it, polishing it, and staring into my blurred reflection, knowing Laszlo had seen his own face staring back from the same watch. I held the watch out to him; it was all I could offer. I had no words, anxious, standing at the edge of a new world, an entire ocean between me and everything I had ever known. My knees shook in the cold

December air. He smiled, took the watch from me, and checked the time.

"Aren't you going to give your cousin a kiss?" he said, at last.

He stepped forward, wrapped his overcoat around me, so we were both enfolded within it, and he kissed me for a long time.

"Welcome home."

Laszlo took me directly to Letourneau's Department Store on Wallace Avenue to buy me some new clothing. I had left my trunk on board the *Amelia* determined to bring nothing of the Old World with me. It was Christmas time, and the windows were full of lights and colorful displays of the season's latest. Smooth-faced mannequins modeled fashions for the coming year, and children pressed their faces against the glass as a toy train chugged its way through a miniature village. A bearded man dressed in red clanged a noisy brass bell outside the front door asking to help the poor. Looking around me at the neon lights, the shiny black cars, and the faces of the smiling shoppers, I could not imagine anyone in America could be poor.

The store was bright and festive, buzzing with activity; salesmen and women rushed back and forth, their arms piled high with boxes. Everyone was in a hurry. Pretty women offered to spray me with the newest perfumes, Black Magic, Evening in Paris, Fleur de Feu, and I let them because I was afraid Laszlo could smell the stink of the ship on me. Before long I must have had four or five different scents on my body because my head began to ache from the sticky sweet smells. I was dizzy with excitement, surrounded by so many different choices of everything. Laszlo told me to choose whatever I wanted, but I did not want to take advantage of his kindness. I tried on hats and scarves and gloves and coats but could decide on nothing.

There was a moving staircase which took us up to the second floor; I had never seen anything like it. In the dress department Laszlo picked out a few dresses he wanted me to try on. The first was a navy blue, silky dress with a tight waist, and pleats. I slipped it on in a small dressing room and emerged feeling like I was putting on a show for Laszlo, who gave a wolf whistle and clapped his hands.

"Aren't you the fashion plate," the salesgirl said with a smile. "Decked out and ready to paint the town." She wore a black gabardine suit dress with small gold buttons on the front and snapped her gum after she spoke.

The dress was very uncomfortable. My skin itched beneath the fabric, and I told Laszlo I did not like it. He asked the salesgirl to wrap it up.

"But it does not feel good," I said.

"It's a good dress," Laszlo said. "It says here it's made of Bemberg silk."

"What is this Bemberg silk?"

"It must be silk from Bemberg," Laszlo said. He turned to the salesgirl, seeking her agreement.

"Bemberg silk is a trade name for rayon," the salesgirl said. "It's a man-made fiber. It's soft and comfortable like silk, it drapes very well, and it won't wrinkle. Care is easy as pie. Just press it with a cool iron between wearings, and you're dynamite."

"I just don't like it one bit," I said, scratching at my shoulder.

"But you have to choose something," Laszlo said. "I don't see what's wrong with this dress."

"What's wrong with it is I don't like it."

The salesgirl, tapped me on the shoulder, interrupted apologetically. "Have you seen our new selection of dresses? Let me show you something made of natural fiber."

"Thank you," I said. "Thank you very much."

I was afraid I had angered Laszlo, but he simply stood aside shaking his head with an amused half smile on his face.

The salesgirl led me over to another rack of dresses. "This one has a longer length skirt. Very 1948. One of our colorful Glentex scarves will contrast with your new dress and highlight the blue." She held up the dress to me, then froze as if she just remembered something important.

"Excuse me madam, do you happen to be German?"

I was ashamed of my greenhorn accent, and had convinced myself at Zeilsheim, the more I tuned in to the Voice of America's regular broadcasts, the more I talked to Betty, the more my accent would disappear. I believed my own lies, but worst of all was the fact this girl, this typical American girl, who snapped her gum and used words like "dynamite" saw in me the most beastly creature anyone could imagine.

"No, no. I'm not German."

"Oh, madam. I'm terribly sorry. I didn't mean to . . ."

I turned my back to her and Laszlo and ran as fast as I could. I reached the moving staircase and stumbled onto it, but the stairs were going the wrong way and the crowd of shoppers shoved me aside like I was a piece of refuse. I must have looked a sight, still dressed in the clothing I wore on the *Amelia*. Tears burst from my eyes, and I could see a mother shielding her children from my sight. When Laszlo reached me, I sobbed, "I want to go home. I want to go home."

Laszlo tried to soothe me in the street outside Letourneau's, where snow had begun to fall, telling me I had traveled a long way and things would feel better in a day or two. "She was a silly young girl. Probably never left Massachusetts in her whole life. You know, by the clueless way I acted around those dresses, she probably thought I was a Martian."

That night, at Laszlo's flat, a small one-room apartment on the second floor of a clapboard house on Story Street, I realized I was going to share a bed with a man for the first time. My heart beat loudly in my chest as I slipped out of my old dress. There was very little furniture. A plain wooden table covered with books and papers, a stack of dirty dishes, a tarnished kettle, and a hot plate sat before one of two windows that looked out onto the dark street. There was a single dining room chair piled with wrinkled clothing, and a small bed that looked like it had been made in a hurry. A cast iron radiator whistled and clanked in the corner. The wallpaper was peeling in places. There was not a womanly touch in the entire apartment. A calendar was nailed to the wall; every day for the past year had a large, penciled X over each day except for today which said "Fannie" in the center of a big circle.

I was afraid I had made a terrible mistake. I could have been on my way to Palestine. At least there, under the warm sun, nobody would mistake me for a German.

Laszlo soothed me, telling me we would move to a nicer place soon. He called me beautiful, his love. When he touched my skin, I forgot all about Palestine.

We were together that night, and it did not have the urgency or the passion I felt the first time in the field outside Zeilsheim. He wore his undershirt and finished quickly, turning out the lights when he was done. "Goodnight Fannie," he said. "I cannot tell you how happy I am to have you here with me."

I lay awake for a long time afterward listening to the sound of his peaceful breathing, the hammer-bang of the radiator, the soft footsteps of a neighbor's midnight-pacing on the ceiling above me.

When I woke in the morning, Laszlo had made me toast and eggs and served them to me in bed.

"You've had a rough time. But that's all over now. I'm going to take care of you."

He had buttered toast for me, and I could see he was trying very hard to please me. "I'll see you tonight," he said. "There's something to eat in the ice box."

"Where are you going?"

"I have to go to work. I already had to fight to take yesterday off. Tonight, I'll take you to the movies," he said.

"But what will I do all day?"

"Enjoy your freedom."

I could not finish my breakfast. A feeling of abandonment filled me, and I sank down under the blanket and stifled a cry. What did I expect? That Laszlo would stay by me all the time and not go to work? I knew so little of the world; I could only imagine the two of us together like we were that night beneath the stars. My legs stirred and I stood up, knowing it was time to walk. Whenever my mind drifted toward a dark place, my legs would take over and I would walk and walk. I didn't know if I was walking to keep the past at bay or to find it.

I found a spare overcoat hanging on a hook by the front door. It smelled of mothballs and cedar. I draped his coat over me and was swallowed up within it like a child. Before long, I had rolled up the sleeves and pinned them, stuffed the shoulders with a pair of scarves, found one of Laszlo's belts and cinched it at the waist, doubling up the bottom of the coat into a tight bundle circling my knees.

I must have looked comical, like a coal-covered snowman marching down Story Street in the frigid sunshine. My breath blew in clouds in front of me. Already the ends of my ears were raw from the cold. I had no key to Laszlo's apartment, and once I started walking, I could not stop until my legs told me it was time. I walked through neighborhoods packed tight with three-story wooden houses, laundry lines stretched out with ghostly frozen undergarments, past snow-covered cars hunched in the road like the forgotten dead, black skeletons of trees waving goodbye in the wind. A distant train whistled somewhere . . .

Walking, walking, walking. My feet are numb and black with red blooms of frostbite. We have been moving for days, sleeping with our eyes open, beaten with clubs as we march west. My father and brother, Chaim, ahead of me, slip now and then in the fresh snow, but never fall. Behind me a man has just been shot after tripping on a frozen ridge of mud. I hear the rifle shot, but do not turn around. The sound of gunfire is more natural to me than the singing of birds, and I have learned to ignore it. I want so much to lie down and close my eyes and sleep forever, but something inside, some burning thing will not let me. I no longer feel my lips, but whisper to myself, "you must live, you must live, you must live." It has been days since we have eaten anything more than snow and dead leaves. Walking, walking, walking, always driven on, night and day.

Beside us a farmer is riding in a wagon pulled by a skinny horse, a dirty gray sunrise at our backs. He has a round, red-cheeked face. In the night, I heard my father rasping and coughing and now that day has broken, I see he has thrown an arm around Chaim for support, his legs weak beneath him. I am afraid they will both be shot. I look in the farmer's eyes and see compassion, understanding, and try to smile at him.

"Komm zu mir."

"My father is not well," I say. "We can't walk anymore."

"Komm zu mir," he says again.

I step out of line and reach for his gloved hand. He pulls me into his wagon and throws a blanket over me. "You are a human being," I say.

His breath smells sour as he leans close to me and tells me I am a "hübsches Mädchen, pretty girl." He touches my cheek with a dirty finger and asks me to lie down in the wagon so no one sees me. Brittle shafts of winter wheat are scattered on the wagon floor. My father and brother keep marching ahead and do not turn around. I explain to the farmer that my father's lungs are bleeding and he cannot walk anymore. "Please let us ride in your wagon."

"First you have to give me something."

"But I do not have anything."

"You do," he says, "You do."

He presses deep between my legs, his belly crushing my ribs. I am only skin and bones and rags. I feel nothing but a dull throbbing pain; I no longer feel shame. I close my eyes the entire time he moves inside me. I smell stale wheat and feel wood splinters in my back and think of my father and brother riding in the wagon, wrapped in blankets. When he is done he wipes himself on me and tells me to get out of the wagon.

"But you said you would let my father and brother ride in the wagon."

He laughs and his face is an entirely different face than the kind, round face I saw before. "Get out or I'll have you shot."

"But my father is ill."

"Your father is an insect and you are a Jewish, insect, whore." He throws me from his wagon.

Walking, walking, walking. I find my father face down in the snow, a halo of blood spreading around his head, but I cannot stop walking.

A police officer found me some time later standing at the edge of the river. It was frozen over and laughing children skated upon its surface. I knew the watch factory was on the Charles River, but I did not see it anywhere. Perhaps this was a different river.

"Are you all right, miss?" the policeman asked. He held his cap in his hand and approached me cautiously. "You were screaming bloody murder."

"I am sorry."

"Are you lost?"

"Yes," I said. "I am lost."

I told him where Laszlo worked, and he put me in his car and drove a short distance to the Walden American Watch and Horologe factory. It was a large, red-brick building, full of tall windows and smokestacks and pointed towers. It looked like a castle or a fortress and took up an entire city block.

When Laszlo found me, sitting inside the warm police car, he took my hand in his and asked me what had happened.

"I was walking," I said.

"In this cold?" Laszlo said.

"I didn't know what else to do."

"Fannie, Fannie," he said shaking his head, "Let's get you home and into a hot bath."

Laszlo drew a bath for me and filled the tub with fragrant bubbles. He sat, fully clothed at the edge of the tub, and asked if he could soap my feet. I sank my scarred and knotted feet deeper beneath the bubbles and said, "I want to get a job."

He laughed and said "I'm going to take care of all your needs. You will never have to worry again. You don't need a job." The bathroom was full of steam and through the mist I could see Laszlo's face was red, and he was sweating.

"But I have worked since I was twelve years old. The raincoat factory in Tarnów . . . I had friends there."

"I don't want you to work."

"Why, Laszlo? I was an excellent tailor at Zeilsheim. My hands were always busy, and I found something like happiness while I worked."

"Because," Laszlo said, "you slaved for the Germans long enough. You should never have to work again for the rest of your life."

"But I want to work," I said, petulantly splashing bathwater at Laszlo. "With a job I can make myself again as an American, a new me." My voice echoed in the bathroom and my voice felt full and deep and strong.

"But the old you is perfect."

"It is not. It is far from perfect."

"Fannie."

"I have a chance to start again."

"And where would you work?" Laszlo said. "At Letourneau's?"

A church bell clanged somewhere, and I turned away like I had been slapped. Did he really think that little of me? "Get out. I want to be alone."

"Look at me," he said.

"Get out, get out, get out."

He did not move from his spot on the edge of the bathtub.

"You think I am worthless."

"Fannie." His voice had softened, and he waited for me to turn back. "I'm sorry," he said. "I shouldn't have brought that up. Sometimes though, work doesn't build you up, it wears you down and makes you sick until . . . And I just can't imagine losing you."

He was quiet for a long time, measuring out his words so they would come out right. "My mother," he said, "worked in the watch factory before I was born. It was her job to paint hands and numbers on the watch faces with glow-in-the-dark paint. She loved going to work with all of her friends, a modern woman with a paycheck. I have a picture of her smiling with painted teeth and lips and cheeks, glowing in the dark like she was magic. My mother was a Radium Girl. The Undark paint the girls used to paint the watches was radioactive. That's why it glowed like it did. Their bosses told them to use their mouths to put a fine point on the brushes after every three or four numbers. My mother painted more than two hundred watches a day, shipped to every corner of the globe. She believed it was important work.

"After I was born, my mother complained about pain and swelling in her jaw. She had horrible bleeding in her gums. Then most of her teeth fell out. One doctor told her she had syphilis, another said she suffered from neurosis and suggested she start smoking cigarettes to calm her nerves. When I was five years old, my mother's lower jaw, swollen to the size of a grapefruit, fell off. She died two weeks later."

I wrapped my arms around my knees and stared at Laszlo for a long time. There are so many different kinds of tragedies. We had both suffered terrible losses; I understood then he was trying to protect me, not deny my wishes.

"But Laszlo, you work in the watch factory."

"I was lucky. Both my parents had worked for the company, and I was trained for over a year as an engineer and a watchmaker in the factory's own school. I am considered a highly skilled worker."

"And I'm not?"

"I'm not saying that."

"I promise I will not work in the watch factory." I said. "But Laszlo, please let me have a job. It will be good for me."

"The war is over, and the men are back at their jobs in the factories. Sometimes there are positions for young women at Indian Rock, the School for Feeble-Minded Boys. But I've heard that place is hell on earth. I could never let you work there."

"I should be a prisoner in your home with nothing all day to do?"

Laszlo was quiet, his face flushed. He removed his hat, ran his fingers through his hair and sighed. "This isn't exactly the way I imagined it," he said. "But here goes." He left the bathroom, and I could hear him moving things around in his room. He returned a moment later, knelt down in a pool of water in front of the bathtub, looked me directly in the face and said, "Fannie, let me make an honest woman of you."

I did not understand what he meant, but I knew he meant something serious from the look on his face. My heart pounded. I *was* an honest woman.

He fished around inside his pocket for a moment and produced a gold ring.

"I want to marry you," he said, slipping the ring onto my pruned finger.

I thought of all the times as a girl, playing with my mother's rings, pretending I was a princess who would one day marry a king, and then later, with my brothers and sisters, wrapping her rings and necklaces as well as our candlesticks and Kiddush cups and most of our foreign currency in cloth and burying everything in the Buczyna Forest. We marked the place with a pointed stick so we could find our treasures again after the war was over.

"You'll have children—we'll have a family. You'll be too busy to work. You will have your hands full at home." Laszlo's smile made my chest hurt.

"I can't, Laszlo," I said, wishing I could disappear. The words were so difficult for me to say I nearly uttered them in Polish. "I can't."

"You can't marry me?" He looked shocked, a stricken look on his face, his Adam's apple bobbing in his throat to stifle a sob. I knew he felt the same way because that was how I felt. I wanted nothing more than to spend the rest of my life with Laszlo. But I was broken in the most painful way, and I was of no use to him.

"I can't," I said, the warm tears streaming down my face hidden by the cheery bath bubbles. "I should have told you sooner, so you could have found someone else at Zeilsheim. I am broken. I am emptied out. I am useless."

"No," Laszlo said. "You are not."

"I am nothing."

"Fannie, you are my lady love. To me, you are everything, everything in the world."

I was silent for a moment, afraid to utter the words that followed. "I will never have children. I can never have children. If you marry me, it will always be just me and you."

If he was disappointed, he never showed it, and he never again mentioned his desire to start a family. He climbed fully clothed into the bathtub and held me tightly in his arms. "Fannie," he said, kissing my neck. "I could not imagine a better life than just me and you."

AN HONEST WOMAN

Laszlo took me to the Riverbend Grand Ballroom at Oaktree Gardens Park on the Charles River which Laszlo said represented "the utmost in refinement and charm." Artie Shaw and his orchestra was playing, and we danced cheek-to-cheek to "Begin the Beguine," and "Stardust." In a sharp sport coat and silk tie, Laszlo was thrilled to be showing me off to the world, a wide, boyish smile pasted to his handsome face. My feet were clumsy at first in my new heels, and I felt out of place as if the entire dancehall knew that I was just a greenhorn who didn't belong among all the glittering glamour. I didn't know from dancing, but Laszlo was patient with me and whispered into my ear to follow his lead, and soon the two of us flowed together like water. I wore a new evening gown he bought for me downtown at Jordan Marsh just for the occasion. He pressed his body close to mine, and I thought I never wanted to be without him again, not even for a minute.

We ate well-done steak and whipped potatoes and green peas and coconut cream pie. I could have ordered anything I wanted. Laszlo asked the waiter for something called a Beefeater Gibson. It was decorated with a pickled pearl onion and Laszlo told me he believed I would like it. I had never had a cocktail before.

"It's the onion," Laszlo said, "that makes the Gibson the superior drink to the martini."

I had no conception of what a martini was supposed to taste like, but I would have listened to Laszlo talk all night. I must have been the luckiest person in the world.

I was living a dream; a simple seamstress from beyond *yenemsvelt* plucked, for no reason I could understand, from the hellish crowding of the displaced persons' camp to be romanced like a starlet by a blue-eyed prince. I did not deserve such love and attention, but I accepted it greedily, guiltily. I knew Laszlo did not have a lot of money, but I accepted everything because it made him happy to believe I was happy.

Afterward, we walked through the grounds of Oaktree Gardens Park, Laszlo's arm around my shoulder, the two of us embraced by the warmth of his rough wool overcoat. It was snowing, and fat flakes fluttered through the air like feathers. We passed the colorful carousel and the penny arcade that was closed up for the season and Laszlo promised to take me on the Ferris wheel in the summer.

"Have you ever been in a canoe before?" Laszlo asked excitedly as we moved down a gradual slope toward the quiet strip of darkness that was the Charles River. "In the summer, there are hundreds of canoes out there, thousands even."

I had read a battered copy of one of Karl May's *Winnetou* novels while at Zeilsheim and there had been plenty of canoes in those pages, but I told Laszlo I had never before been in a canoe. I then recalled how seasick I had been as I traveled on the *Amelia*, but I said nothing of that to Laszlo. The Gibson had warmed my belly and loosened my tongue so I asked Laszlo how he came to find me, a half a world away when he had everything one could ever want right outside his door.

"Not everything, Fannie."

"You came all the way to Germany to find me, yet you were here in the war. Perhaps if you were already in Germany, I might understand how it was possible that we met."

Laszlo told me that as a master watchmaker he was more valuable doing research and development on military navigational apparatuses than being just another pair of boots on the ground. He was contracted from a local company called Raytheon to work on bombsights that were to be used in B-52 bombers. He explained in great detail how a bombsight has to estimate the path the bomb will take after being dropped from the aircraft, all the while considering wind speed, gravity, and air drag.

"I mainly worked on the new tachometric bombsights that combined with radar systems to allow the aircraft to accurately pinpoint its target through clouds and at night. I like to think that I did more than my part in helping to win the war. But that's not the way people saw it here in Walden."

Since Laszlo was not allowed to talk about his top-secret work, so many of his friends and acquaintances thought that he was avoiding the war, making excuses so he didn't have to go overseas and fight.

"They called me yellow. They called me unpatriotic. Prank callers phoned my house asking to speak to the man of the house and screamed that I was no man when I responded."

It wasn't until after the war and strict secrecy no longer mattered that the truth finally came out how hard Laszlo had worked in doing his part to liberate Europe and to defeat Imperial Japan. Local women who had avoided him and gossiped about the cowardly watchmaker were interested in going on dates with him. But it was too late. The war years had been lonely and often humiliating, but Laszlo had always kept his business secret. "One of the bombsights I helped develop was on the Enola Gay. That made me a bit of a local hero, but it was too late for me to consider forgiving what folks said about me."

I knew there was no purpose in measuring one's pain against another's, because Laszlo's pain was his pain, and my pain was my pain, and true pain can never be explained to another in full measure. But I knew from the tears in Laszlo's eyes that he had suffered and that he had been hurt, and his hurt squeezed at my heart until I, too, hurt.

I told Laszlo I loved him, and he said, "Thank you for loving me."

And I responded, "Thank *you* for loving me."

We kissed there in the snow with the flakes falling all around us like angels leaping from the heavens to witness our love.

We stood at the edge of the Charles River swaddled together inside Laszlo's warm coat. The river was still, frozen over in places, and I recalled as a small girl, in the years before the formation of the ghetto, skating on a frozen pond with my friend Zipora and how much fun the two of us had making patterns in the ice racing around with our borrowed skates. I no longer permitted myself to think of her, so I asked Laszlo how he ended up in Germany after the war, on that unlikely path to meeting me.

He told me that after all that business during the war with people thinking he was ducking out on his patriotic duty, he had a "bee in his bonnet," to get to Germany and do something to help people. "When I learned that the United Nations Relief and Rehabilitation Administration had saved tens of thousands of Jews during the war and was helping out survivors at displaced persons' camps in Germany and elsewhere, I offered up myself for a six month stretch as a kind of mechanical expert who could fix anything and everything with a manual in hand, and most without the manual. And some," Laszlo laughed, "with my eyes closed. I got the job. And the rest, as they say, is history."

Laszlo leaned down to kiss me and I kissed him back, and then I stopped and said, "But why me? What was it about me, a raggedy scarecrow who barely knew English?"

"Fannie," Laszlo said, taking my face in his hands. "Because it was you. And nobody else in this wide world is you, besides you."

"But why me?" I said. "I am not much, and I was even less then."

"You are everything, Fannie."

Out of the corner of my eye, I saw something moving in the darkness on the water where the ice had melted away, and I was frightened and clung to Laszlo. "What is that?"

And then out of the falling snow, like magic, we could both see a pair of swans floating one after the other before us, their curved necks forming a heart as the trailing swan approached the first swan, as if they were putting on a display for the two of us.

"That's us," Laszlo said, squeezing my hand.

"What do you mean?"

"They're swans. Once they're together, they bond for life, and me and you—we are bonded for life as well."

At that moment, I began to cry. I did not think that I could ever be this happy, that a man such as Laszlo could actually be mine for the rest of my life.

"Don't cry," Laszlo said. "I have big plans for us. Ever since I was a little boy, I have wanted to have my own shop. And one day, I'm going to buy my own shop in Walden and sell watches and clocks and fix peoples' watches and clocks. And people will come from all over to buy my watches and clocks because nobody knows more about watches and clocks than me."

It was true that Laszlo knew much about watches and clocks, and it was also true that there were parts of me that Laszlo would never know as long as the two of us lived.

"And then, Fannie, I will buy you a big house in the Heights or a mansion on Cronin's Pond. And you will have everything."

"But what will I do in that big house?"

Laszlo smiled at me, "Darling, you won't have to do anything at all."

While Laszlo went to work long hours at the factory, Temple B'nai Israel became my lifeline. In the days and weeks that followed, I joined the temple's sewing circle, the Sisterhood, and the Book of the Month Club. Sometimes we played mah-jongg and bridge, making penny bets. A few of the ladies spoke Yiddish, American Yiddish they had learned from their parents, and sprinkled it throughout their speech like salt and pepper; one spoke some Russian, another Polish, and nobody ever questioned me about my accent. I quickly familiarized myself with American idioms and expressions, testing phrases with an amused Laszlo at home, one day pouting out my lips and saying, "What's cooking, sugar daddy?"

"Why don't you bring that kisser of yours over here baby doll and find out."

I was welcomed by everybody, part of a large extended family. The Sisterhood was more than just a social club. Sometimes in the temple's kitchen, we would cook or bake and bring meals to the bedridden and the elderly. We arranged dances, held rummage sales to benefit the Sunday school, and raised money for the Jews of Europe still living in displaced persons' camps. But there was gossip and slanderous talk as well—whose husband had gotten a raise, and whose was going to be fired, who was having trouble in bed, and who came home with lipstick on his collar. When I heard Sylvia Rosen say Mae Levin dressed like a DP, I understood their kindness toward others did not always apply to each of us. Sometimes I looked at my new friends and wondered what they said about me when I was not around. If Rose Simon walked like a hooker, and Etta Greenblatt, vice president of the Sisterhood smelled of body odor, I was afraid to imagine what they said about me.

Most mornings, Laszlo and I walked together to the synagogue where he would sit in the cold chapel and join the minyan to say Kaddish for the dead before heading to work at the factory. One sunny morning in March, Laszlo noticed my ring was missing. I told him I had lost it somewhere; it must have slipped from my finger and fallen in the snow. The look of anguish on his face almost caused me to tell him I had removed the ring and buried it beneath one of our apartment's loose floorboards. But I couldn't do it. It was the first of many lies.

"You still want to get married, don't you?" Laszlo asked.

"Of course, I want to marry you. We don't need a ring to get married."

"Yes we do," Laszlo said. "I'll make sure I get you another one, a better one."

Laszlo and I married on May 14, 1948, the same joyous day the State of Israel came into being. I am certain the entire synagogue joined us to celebrate, not just our wedding, but a new and promising future for the entire Jewish people. Etta Greenblatt held one corner of my wedding chuppah and called me sister. Rose Simon, who had given me her lace dress and veil, whispered advice into my ear about proper behavior on one's wedding night. Grandfatherly Rabbi Kirshenblatt inscribed for me a copy of *Man's Search for Meaning*, by Viktor Frankl, wishing me a long and prosperous life. There were fireworks, catered food, live music, and lots of dancing late into the night. Laughing children waved tiny blue-and-white homemade flags with crooked, hand-drawn Stars of David in the center. Moses Cahn, the temple president and owner of Cahn's Superior Liquors, provided the alcohol and shook everyone's hand as he passed out cigars to the men. I must have been quite drunk, because I felt, as I was carried aloft through the brightly lit ballroom on a plush chair, that if I jumped from my cloud chair, I would be caught in someone's arms. This was a new sensation for me, and I looked down at the blurred smiling faces and wept with joy.

We moved out of Laszlo's bachelor apartment to a proper one-bedroom apartment on the third floor on Story Street. The men of the Brotherhood said they would carry our few sticks of furniture up the narrow staircase to our new home. But they did more than that, and surprised us, pooling their money together to buy us a brand-new bed and a pair of white Hudson's Bay point blankets Morris Davids had purchased on a trip to Canada.

There were so many simchas in those days, so much to celebrate with the world returning to normal, and sometimes it felt almost like the past years had been nothing more than a terrible nightmare. Every week there were two or three weddings or bar mitzvahs. There were baby namings and Brit Milahs and Kiddush luncheons almost every day.

It was fortunate for Laszlo he did not stay after minyan for the circumcision of Moses Cahn's baby boy Jacob, but his decision not to attend changed everything in my life. Laszlo was not afraid of blood, unless it was coming from a baby's thing and he avoided Brit Milahs like a sickness. The mohel who performed the procedure must have made a bad cut somewhere, because blood was everywhere, on the cushion upon which the wailing baby rested, on the floor and on the front of the terrified mohel's white shirt. Two or three women fainted on the spot and Moses Cahn roared, "Is there a goddamn doctor in the house?"

The wretched mohel dipped a wine-soaked finger in the baby's mouth, but it continued to cry. Someone told the mohel to apply pressure to the wound and the bleeding would stop, but he was too afraid to touch the baby and backed away muttering some sort of prayer through his beard. I grabbed some napkins off the luncheon table and pressed my hands over the wound, careful not to push too hard on his little body. His cry was like that of an animal caught in a trap. I wanted so badly to take away the pain, I would have done anything to help the poor child. It had no understanding it was surrounded by loved ones. I had seen that terrified face many times before and had been helpless to stop it. I held him at my breast and pressed him to my heart. Without intending to do so, I began to sing a popular song I knew from the theater back in Krakow. I sang very slowly and rocked him in my arms:

Sheyn vi di levone,
You are as beautiful as the moon,
Likhtik vi di shtern,
you are as bright as the stars,
Fun himl a matone,
sent to me from the heavens,

Bistu mir tzugeshikt.
you are a gift from above.
Mayn glik hob ikh gevunen,
I found my happiness when I saw you.
Ven ikh hob dikh gefunen,
You made my heart happy,
Sheyn vi toyznt zunen
you are as beautiful
Hot mayn hartz baglikt.
as a thousand suns.

Before I had even finished singing, the baby stopped crying and had fallen asleep, his perfect bald head cradled in my arms. I removed the napkins and the blood had stopped flowing. Moses Cahn snatched the baby from me without a word of thanks and handed it to its mother who bathed him in kisses and disappeared into the privacy of the temple library to tend to her only child.

"All right, let's eat," someone said. "There's plenty of food for everyone."

"That was gorgeous," Etta Greenblatt said to me. She held a plate of smoked salmon, herring, and chopped egg in her hand. She popped a pickled caper into her mouth. "You sound just like the Barry Sisters."

"Thank you," I said.

"Oh, you'll make such a wonderful mother one day."

The ladies' room was downstairs from the function hall beside a pair of pay telephones with small, stenciled signs asking worshippers to refrain from making phone calls on Shabbas. From an alcove, I heard a pair of voices echoing off the bare walls and the smooth terrazzo floor. "I should cut your balls off after what you pulled today."

"It was an honest mistake. My hand slipped."

"Well, here's another honest mistake for you to think about."

I heard grunts and moans and what sounded like a sack of flour being dropped to the ground.

"Oops. It looks like my hand slipped too."

"I didn't mean to."

"Get up and take your medicine like a man."

"Mr. Cahn, I'm sorry. I apologize. Your baby will be fine." The mohel had a high-pitched pleading voice "He won't remember a thing." He stammered out something like a laugh.

"Do you know how this looks? Do you? My only son Jack nearly became Jacqueline because you couldn't keep your hand still. He'll be a laughingstock if people find out. I asked for a mohel, and I got a shohet. You slaughterer, you rotten excuse for a man. Get up on your feet."

"No."

"Don't say I didn't warn you."

I had slipped quietly down the stairs and sat on the bottom step trying to get a better look at what was happening. Moses Cahn was not tall, maybe five foot seven or eight and maybe fifty years old. His hair had not yet started to gray. He was built like a wine barrel, broad across the chest with short, powerful arms and legs. Moses Cahn, red in the face and dressed in his double-breasted, brown pinstripe suit, looked like vengeance itself as he kicked the hapless mohel again and again in the face, the stomach, the legs.

"Get up, Schmulewitz, you coward."

I had seen so much violence in my life that had sickened me, caused me to deny the very existence of God, one might have expected me to feel revulsion at what I saw—a man's face being kicked into a bloody pulp—but I felt no such thing. Instead, I felt a sort of justice was taking place before my eyes. When Moses Cahn was finished, Schmulewitz lay barely conscious on the ground, writhing in his own blood. "I'll send you a bill. Now go home and clean yourself up, you useless momzer."

The mohel, Schmulewitz, stumbled past me without even looking in my direction; one of his eyes was sealed shut, his crooked nose broken.

"Don't forget to take your teeth," Moses Cahn called after him, tossing a pair of bloodied teeth like a set of dice.

I didn't know what to say, so I simply said, "Mazel tov on the birth of your son."

Moses Cahn licked the blood from his knuckles and many-ringed fingers like a jungle beast after battle. He was out of breath, and he looked surprised to see me.

"You're the one who sang "Beautiful as the Moon," to little Jack."

"Yes," I said, surprised he had recognized a song from my youth. "You speak Yiddish?"

"A *bisl*," he said smiling. "I saw Bessie Thomashevsky sing it once at the Folksbiene in New York City." His face was dark, handsome with thick, black eyebrows and a sharp nose. He wore his coal-black hair brushed straight back on his head. He had a cleft chin and looked like he needed a shave.

"That business didn't upset you, did it?"

"Not at all," I said. "He hurt your baby."

"You hire a professional and you expect results."

"He did not do his job properly," I said.

"Most of these stiffs here call me Moses," he said extending a bloody hand to shake. "But you can call me Moe."

"I am Fannie. You gave out cigars at my wedding."

Moses Cahn looked puzzled, and then remembered, and his face became bright. "Independence Day. The bride was you?"

"Yes," I said. "I'm married to Laszlo Schwartz. He is a watchmaker."

Moses Cahn was not familiar with Laszlo. Perhaps he only knew his face but could not match it to his name. "Since the war, he says Kaddish every day for the dead. The camps, Hiroshima. He feels responsible to ease the pain in their souls."

"You don't believe in that horseshit."

"I don't believe in anything."

"Well, that's good," he said.

He was looking at me, and there was something about his eyes that frightened me, the way they looked not at me, but into me.

"You're not wearing a wedding ring," he said.

"No," I said. "I've lost two rings already. My fingers are very slim, and we can't afford to buy another."

Moses Cahn stepped closer and took my hands in his, turning them over and inspecting the palms tenderly with a battered index finger. "You don't work."

"I am busy at the synagogue."

Then he noticed the numbers on my arm. "Where?"

I told him where I had been during those years, and he simply shook his head sadly. "You're from Poland."

I was not comfortable talking about my past, so I said. "You have a beautiful boy."

"He'll do just fine if he survives what that butcher did. Besides that, ten fingers, ten toes, everything in the right place."

We were both quiet for a moment. I could hear chairs being dragged across the floor above our heads. "So, you're not working," he said, "but, you're not having a baby."

I was surprised he would say such a thing having just met me.

"How do you know?" I said.

"Are you having a baby? Ever?"

"No," I said after a long moment.

"The way you rocked little Jack in your arms and sang to him. I think you would have kept him for your own."

"Stop it," I said. "I did not like to see him cry. I only tried to soothe him."

"Because you've seen enough children suffer?"

"Stop it," I said.

"Because you couldn't stop their pain?"

"Enough," I said.

"What do you do to ease your pain? Volunteer with a bunch of yentas? You deserve more."

From upstairs, a voice called out, "Has anyone seen Moses? I've looked everywhere."

"Listen," he said. "I think I understand what you need. This is America. Make something of yourself, make some money for yourself, and buy yourself a new ring, a handful of rings. You're not like the rest of the yentas here."

He handed me a beige business card that was warm from his hand. "Come by my office and talk to me. I think I've got something for you to do."

After he left, I realized my heart had been thumping so hard I needed to sit down and catch my breath. I looked at the card which read: CAHN'S SUPERIOR LIQUORS—MOSES CAHN, PROPRIETOR. The back of the card was smudged with the mohel's blood.

I did not tell Laszlo I had spoken with Moses Cahn, nor did I tell Laszlo three days later I was going to meet Moses Cahn at his office at the liquor store. I did not know what he could have had in mind for me, but I felt anticipation building as I walked along Wallace Avenue. That person walking beside me in the shop windows, reflected from the glass, was a vision of me I had not seen in a long time, my arms swinging at my sides, a tiny smile playing on my lips. I wore a pretty polka-dotted dress Laszlo had bought for me to save for a special occasion.

Moses Cahn greeted me with a cheerful, "There she is," as he rose from his swivel chair. He had a fat cigar between his teeth and wore a shirt open at his thick neck.

He sat at the other side of a large wooden desk, cluttered with papers and notebooks and bottles. He offered me a drink. "Anything you want. Thirty-year single malt, Russian vodka, Green Chartreuse *and* Yellow, we've got it all. This is the most fully stocked liquor store between Boston and Hartford. Opened the day after Prohibition. We'll close when the Messiah comes." He laughed, not like a fifty-year-old man, but like a child amusing himself.

I thanked him and declined his offer.

"Your husband doesn't know you're here."

"No."

He smiled, "And the yentas?"

"No."

"To courage," he said. "And to being your own person."

He poured me a drink anyway and I drank it because I was nervous. It burned all the way down my throat and set fire to my belly. I had not eaten breakfast that morning.

"I'm a businessman," he said leaning forward in his chair. "And an important community leader. I've got my finger in a lot of pies: liquor, real estate, the stock market, and some things I'd rather not talk about. Ever since my brother Nat died last year, I've been looking for someone I can trust to help me out with one of my businesses. Can I trust you?"

"Yes."

"I know I can, Fannie." His brown eyes sent a warning in his look. "It's very simple. Twice a week I need you to pick up something for me. There are four stops on Wallace Avenue, two on Main Street and one at the shoemaker on Monticello Street."

I did not know what to say, so I remained silent.

"Then all you have to do is take the commuter train downtown to the North End and drop off the packages at Benvenuto's Bakery. Have you ever tasted their pignoli?"

"No."

"Most delicious pastries in the world."

He removed a fat billfold from his pocket and peeled off three fifty-dollar bills. "I'll pay you a hundred and fifty dollars a week. Besides that, the less you know, the better."

The bills felt smooth in my hands, like the dry skin of a long-lost loved one. "An advance for your services."

"Why me?" I asked.

"This can be a dangerous business. You'll be handling a lot of money for me. My brother had a reputation, and nobody was ever late when he came to pick up the envelope. You know the saying 'live by the sword...?' Well, he's gone now, and I need you to help me. You're not afraid of me, are you?"

"No," I said.

He laughed and stubbed out his cigar in an ashtray. "I'm just a big teddy bear," he said, spreading his arms wide. "The danger is out there. But nobody, nobody in the world would ever expect you to be working for me. If someone corners you in Walden, just give them a taste of your greenhorn accent. Tell them you don't speak English. Once you're in the North End, the Marinos have their people everywhere. You couldn't be safer in the Vatican."

"All right," I said. "Just pick up and drop off? I can do that."

"Good. You're working for me now. Let me show you your route," he said unrolling a map of downtown Walden. He dropped a heavy finger on a small red x at the south end of Wallace Avenue. "The Shebeen. You start here and walk north toward Main Street. Just make sure nobody is following you. Now put your money away and buy yourself something nice."

The Shebeen was a gloomy Irish pub that smelled of sour beer and the unwashed bodies of men. It took a moment for my eyes to adjust to the darkness after walking in the sunshine of Wallace Avenue. Neon signs advertising Schlitz and Narragansett Lager flickered and hummed. Two or three men sat at the bar drowsily nursing pint glasses, with empty expressions on their pale faces. A heavyset man wiping glasses with a dirty rag asked me what I wanted.

I had rehearsed the lines again and again as I readied myself that morning, but I was still afraid I would lose my nerve or say the wrong thing. He asked me again what I wanted, and this time the men at the bar looked up from their glasses. "Moe sent me," I said, my voice squeezed by nerves.

"Feck off. You think I'm thick, do ye? Now leg it out of here before I lose my cool."

"Moe sent me," I said again. "I'm picking something up."

He draped the rag over his shoulder, fixed his eyes on me, and laughed, "So your man's got a new bagman, does he. Well that just takes the cake. A sheeny and a woman both."

Moses Cahn told me to never say more than I need to say, but I said, "I'll tell him you said hello."

"Is that supposed to be some sort of lousy threat?" His two front teeth were missing, and he explored the empty space with his tongue.

"No," I said. "I would just like to get what I came for."

"And what did ye come for?" he said, raising his eyebrows suggestively, as he stepped around the bar. He flicked open a knife blade and held it to my neck.

"Is this what ye came for?"

"No," I said.

He pressed the knife against my skin, and I stared forward, not blinking my eyes. There had been many times in my life I had been prepared to die, but as I stared at myself in the greasy mirror above the bar, I knew I would do anything to live if only the man asked me. My life with Laszlo had just begun, and I could feel the promise of a future for the first time ever. The blade was cold, and I could smell his sickly sour breath close to my face. I did not dare move, and for a long time, minutes perhaps, the bartender did not move either. My eyes were becoming dry, and I was afraid if I blinked them, he would cut me. But just when I thought I could not hold out any longer, he removed the knife from my neck, folded it up and slipped it into his pocket.

"Your nerves must be made of iron. Here ye go," he said sliding a paper bag along the bar. "My regards to Moe. Tell him he can expect no trouble here."

In the street, I threw myself over the hood of a car and wept until my lungs hurt. I thought I had left the world of death and near death behind me. I considered running as fast as I could to the watch factory and throwing myself into Laszlo's arms. But I could not be with him all the time, and I needed to make a life for myself. The paper bag in my hand represented a future that would be mine alone, something I could share with no one, not even Laszlo. My feet began to walk even before my mind told them to do so and I made my way quickly down Wallace Avenue and away from the bartender and The Shebeen, a cool breeze erasing the touch of the blade from my skin.

My next stop was Brennan's Hardware two blocks to the north. I made the pickup without any incident at both the hardware store and The Frosty Head, another bar that was much cheerier than The Shebeen. At Jimmy's Barbershop on the Common, four or five men sat around smoking cigarettes and laughing. One overweight man sat in the barber chair getting a shave from a mustached man dressed in a white smock. "The morning line had Gone West at fifteen to one, a beautiful homebred chestnut, a stretch runner who finished off the board his last three races. But he's got pedigree, and I heard whispers from his trainer he was due to finish in the money. I seen him run at Suffolk last spring and knew the smart money was on Gone West. Pennies from heaven, you'd think."

The fat man spoke with a thick local accent, and I had difficulty deciphering some of his words. "So, I put $500 on him to win, and would you believe by post time he'd been bet down to three to five.

"And did he win?" One of the men asked blowing smoke rings into the air.

"Yeah, he won. But I lost a bundle, and now I have some explaining to do with the wife."

"You know scared money never wins."

"But Gone West won the race," the man said. "He led wire to wire, and I got left in the dust."

The men finally noticed me standing in the doorway. One of them wolf-whistled at me and said something I'd rather not repeat. I asked to speak with Jimmy.

"I'm Jimmy," the man in white said.

"I'd like to speak to you in private."

The men hooted and hollered and made rude comments as Jimmy and I stepped behind the curtain that led to a small storage room piled high with boxes of Barbasol and Brylcreem. "Moe sent me," I said.

He smiled a kind smile. "It's you? Moe is always full of surprises."

Jimmy found a paper bag bundled inside a cardboard box. He slipped it into my net shopping bag with the rest of my pickups. Jimmy squeezed my shoulder in a friendly way. "We don't need to speak. Just come in the delivery door out back, take your package, and be on your way. It will always be in there between the jars of Barbicide." He pushed the curtain aside, winked at me and said, "Good luck."

TRUST, BUT VERIFY

I never imagined I could ever be anything but thin. I had known deprivation for so long, I was certain my body had been carved down to its essentials. But as the years went on and I deposited my packages at Benvenuto's Bakery, leaving my paper sack behind the display case counter in exchange for an identical paper bag full of the most wonderful pastries, I saw my body change from skinny and angled to plump and shapely. Laszlo loved my new body, and he buried his face in my breasts, and slapped me playfully on the behind, and kissed me behind the ears. I felt with each pound I gained, the further I got from death. It was as if each pound were deposited in a bank to be saved against a future catastrophe.

Outside the bakery that first time, clutching the bag in my arms, I felt guilty to hold in my embrace such a warm sweet-smelling bag of treats. I was instructed to walk down Hanover Street to North Station with the replacement bag in my arms in case somebody suspicious happened to be following me. I was certain nobody had noticed me slip in and out of Benvenuto's crowded bakery. The pastries smelled so delicious. What was I to do with them all? I knew I should share them with the Sisterhood, who welcomed me, taught me how to play mah-jongg and how to apply makeup to help fill out my lips. But something told me I needed to eat everything in the bag, not just for me, but for my brothers and sisters and parents who had known such hunger. I ducked down a narrow alleyway and selected a sweet cannoli off the top. I devoured it in two bites and grabbed another from the bag and ate it just as quickly, the rich ricotta cheese melting on my tongue. Before long, my chin and fingers were covered in confectioner's sugar and flaking crumbs of buttery pastry crust. I could not eat fast enough. There in the alleyway beside the trash barrels overtopped with the week's refuse, I ate more than a dozen cannolis, crunchy pignolis, sfogliatelle, sweet cream puffs, and two or three biscotti which tasted even better than my own mother's homemade mandelbrodt.

As I devoured those delicious sweets and delights, my heart began to race, sweat forming at my brow. I was very thirsty, my tongue thick with paste. I knew my stomach was full but could not stop eating. My head throbbed behind my eyes and everything around me blurred and I was spinning, spinning, spinning.

When I came to, I found myself on the ground, the putrid taste of vomit in my mouth. A man with a round, friendly face, a thin mustache, and a broad-brimmed hat stood over me. He reached into his suit pocket and produced a handkerchief. What humiliation I felt, kneeling in my own vomit as I took the embossed handkerchief from his outstretched hand. His fingernails were newly manicured, and his shoes were shined to a bright glaze. The initials A.M. were embroidered in a grand script at the corner of the garment, and I knew immediately he was one of the Marino brothers. I realized later he must have been watching me from his offices above the bakery; he had seen me enter and exit, but when he did not see me appear on Hanover Street, he became worried something happened to me. I'm sure he could have never imagined what I had done to myself, eating all those pastries to the point of sickness. A sly look of relief crossed his face, his black eyes twinkling. I offered him the handkerchief back and he took it from me, not caring about the mess I had made of it. He folded it carefully and slipped it into his pocket. He smiled and offered me his hand. It was soft and smooth, and small for a man.

"Next time don't eat so much," he said.

"I won't," I said. "They were so delicious."

He had a thin pale scar across the entire length of his neck, and he noticed me noticing it.

"Here," he said, handing me a crisp ten-dollar bill. "Take a cab home and clean yourself up."

Later, when I reported to Moses Cahn in his office, he said, "There's my girl Friday." He asked me to have a seat and poured me a drink. I refused the drink and he frowned. "I heard you had a little one-on-one with Tony Marino."

"Yes. He was very kind," I said.

"Kind is a funny word to describe a Marino."

Moses Cahn drained his glass and stared hard at me, hungrily. "Be careful with those guinea cut throats. You're liable to make me jealous."

"Aren't you in business with the Marinos?" I said, not understanding his hostility.

"Let's just say we've come to an arrangement that is equitable for both sides. For now. The Marinos and me are both in the laundry business, but those wop cocksuckers are bleeding me dry. Don't forget, Fannie, we'll never be more than money grubbing Christ-killers to them. That's why folks like us need to stick together."

One might wonder how Laszlo never knew what I was doing all those years. I was making more money than he was at the watch factory and only joined the ladies of the Sisterhood a few days a week. I knew I could not spend the money on clothing or new furnishings for our apartment; even a Friday night brisket would draw his suspicion. It was my responsibility to do the weekly food shopping, but our budget never allowed for the slightest extravagance with the watch factory struggling and workers being laid off.

As the weeks passed and the money piled up, buried secretly beneath our floorboards with my two wedding rings, I worried all that money could at any moment become worthless like so much colored confetti. I needed to have that money available quickly in case the madness of Europe ever found its way to America.

When I was very small, my father showed me a Weimar Republic fifty-million-mark banknote he had received in the mail from a friend in Germany who had wallpapered his study with the useless bills. It was such a serious looking bill with lots of German writing filling up the space beneath the word "Reichsbanknote," a red "50" suspended in the background. I thought the two identical black eagles caged in tight circles at the bottom of the note looked like brave chickens flexing their muscles. My family quickly adapted from the once-stable Polish złoty to the new ghetto currency, the banknote stamped on both sides with a six-pointed star and the Nazi Swastika, but outside the ghetto, it was worthless. I knew from the most painful experience nothing at all retained its value like gold and that gold was the only currency acceptable everywhere in the world. I hurried home, afraid I would be too late, fearing the US dollar had suddenly lost all its worth, and I could not, if needed, book passage to a safe country. In our apartment, I called out Laszlo's name in case he had come home sick, and then I checked the bathroom and our small kitchen to make sure nobody was hiding behind a door. Then I knelt on the wood floor and pried back the floorboard, breaking a fingernail, and reached into the darkness, my heart pounding . . .

"I can't find it," Chaim says. "We buried it right here under this tree."

"But all the trees look the same without their leaves," I say.

It is almost dark, and I can barely make out the crooked Star of David sewn onto my brother's new armband. We have been digging in the frozen soil for nearly an hour with soup spoons we stole from our kitchen. When we buried mother's jewels and the rest of our family valuables it was late summer and the ground was fragrant and soft and the trees were in joyous bloom. It was a game of treasure hunt, and we knew nobody would ever find our prize except us. We felt so proud of our secret, and that we had outsmarted the Germans. Now, in the hard earth beneath the skeletal ash trees, we are lost.

Chaim begins to cry in frustration. "It's supposed to be right here. We buried it right here."

Buczyna Forest for the first time looks frightening, forbidding. The bones of the trees sway back and forth in the wind and offer no protection from the elements.

"If we don't turn in our gold, all of our valuable possessions, they will kill us."

I laugh a nervous laugh. Who has ever heard of something so ridiculous? It is our gold, and we should be allowed to keep it, if only we can find it.

"But Chaim—"

My words are interrupted by a gunshot in the distance and Chaim's face melts in a display of terror.

"Keep digging," he shouts.

There was a small pawn shop on Wallace Avenue. Its dark, crowded windows were full of violins, bongo drums, grandfather clocks, mink stoles, a brass samovar, and countless other items that had once meant so much to their owners. I entered through a discrete side door and rang a small bell on the cluttered counter. A half-eaten ham sandwich sat in wax paper wrapping beside an ashtray that smoked with a live cigarette. A middle-aged man appeared after a moment and pulled a wire cage across the length of the counter, separating the two of us.

"How can I help you?" he asked. He sounded very bored.

He wore a brown sweater-vest over a rumpled white shirt and was thin with a long nose and long nicotine-yellowed fingers.

"I'd like to buy some gold jewelry."

"What do you have in mind?"

"I don't have anything special in mind."

"All right," he said, as if the weight of the entire world rested upon his shoulders. "We've got rings, necklaces, bracelets, earrings, brooches, hat pins, cufflinks. This is where dreams come to die. We've got everything. Now just tell me what you are interested in."

"I am interested in everything."

"Everything?" He sucked on his cigarette and eyed me with suspicion.

"Everything that is gold."

He smiled. "If you've got the Jack, I can help you out."

I removed six hundred dollars from my pocketbook and placed it on the counter between us. His eyebrows jumped and his narrow eyes rounded in his head.

"You don't want to carry a wad like that around. Someone's liable to jump you for that kind of dough."

"I plan on spending it all here."

He laughed, or rather snorted, and lit a new cigarette from the end of his old one. He took a long suck on it, held the smoke inside for a long moment, and then blew it out the side of his mouth. He extended his hand to me and said with a lopsided smile, "You're always welcome to spend your money here."

Then he double-locked the front door and flipped over the CLOSED sign. He rushed around the shop, emptying glass display cases, gathering up all the gold he could find, and spreading it out before me on the worn counter. "Where should we start?" he said. "Rings? Necklaces? What are you most interested in?"

"I am interested in twenty-four karats, eighteen karats, and fourteen karats. As long as it is gold, I want to buy it."

"We've got coins as well. Do you like coins? Take a look-see at this." He fished around in his pants pocket and placed a shining gold piece between us. A stern-looking Indian in a feathered headdress showed himself in profile underneath the word "Liberty."

"This is a 1909 Indian Head five-dollar gold coin. Pick it up and feel it. There is no other US coin like it. Look at that raised design. Look at the details of the Indian chief, how they are sunk right into the surface of the gold. That's a quarter troy ounce of fine gold." He picked the coin up in his long fingers and bit down on it. "This is the real McCoy," he said. "And I've got more in the safe out back."

"Your test for gold is simply to bite the coin? There must be some other test. I am going to be spending a lot of money on gold, and I cannot take the risk it is not real."

"Lady, I'm not trying to rip you off."

"I believe it is important to trust, but also to verify."

"Are you calling me a liar?"

"No," I said. "But there are many places I can spend my money," I said, snatching my bills off the counter. "I want to know for certain what I am buying is gold."

"All right, all right" he said, checking the time on his wristwatch and rolling up his shirt sleeves. "Now pay attention." He produced a dull piece of white tile from beneath the counter and laid it flat. Then he selected a plain gold wedding band and held it up for me to see. From behind the wire cage, his green eye blinked inside the circle.

"If this is real gold, there will be a yellow streak when I rub it on the porcelain tile. If it makes a black streak, then it's pyrite, and worthless. Fool's gold." The pawnbroker ran the edge of the ring along the tile and behind it appeared a golden-yellow streak like a comet. "See," he said. "Simple. This is gold."

He slid the ring forward. I held the ring in my hand and even for a moment slipped it onto my finger. My hand trembled and I removed it.

"Now," the pawnbroker said, holding up a u-shaped magnet. "Hold the magnet near the ring." He handed me the battered horseshoe magnet through the opening in the cage. I held them several inches apart. The gold wedding band pulled closer, the invisible magnetic field drawing the ring into its grasp.

His long fingers snatched the ring from my hand. "This," he said. "Is not pure gold. There are other metals mixed in here. If it's pure gold, the magnet will not attract it. Remember: precious metals are not magnetic."

"How would you know how many karats the ring is?"

"Boy, are you getting your money's worth and more today—a free lesson in metallurgy."

"I never said anything about free. If I am happy, I will come back again and again to your shop."

"Since you'll be a return customer, you might as well know my name," he said thoughtfully. "I'm Smith."

"Pleasure to meet you Mr. Smith."

"You're not from around here."

"It does not matter where I'm from."

"I was born and raised right here in Walden. Went to Walden High—"

"That is very nice," I said. "But I would like to buy some gold."

"Suit yourself," he said. "There's one more test you want to know. I'll be right back."

Smith returned a few minutes later from a cluttered back room. He was drying a small square of black stone with a handkerchief. "To test the value of gold, you need a testing stone and acids. He flipped the latch on a small wooden box that had been sitting the entire time right before me on the counter. Inside the box were several small bottles. Smith told me they contained different strengths of testing acid. He plucked a thin needle out of a slot in the box and showed me its gold tip.

"Let's get the goods on this bracelet."

He handed me a chain-link gold bracelet with a square clasp and asked me how many karats it was.

I studied the bracelet, fingering the links nervously, rubbing the gold to feel its texture and softness between my fingers. But I could not determine how many karats it was, or even if it was in fact gold.

"Look under the clasp," Smith said. "Is anything stamped there? Most commercial gold is marked. Not always correctly, mind you. With gold valued at thirty-five dollars an ounce, somebody's always going to try and cheat you if they can."

I turned over the bracelet. "It says '18 K.'"

"All right," he said, lifting a small bottle of acid out of the box. "Trust, but verify." He smiled and his gold tooth twinkled.

Smith asked me to scratch the bracelet along the testing stone. He snapped on a pair of rubber gloves. Then he placed a drop of acid on the gold streak I had just made, and within seconds it began to disappear.

He whistled and shook his head. "Fibber McGee and Molly. Somebody's not telling the truth. If that's eighteen karats, I'm Pope Pius XII."

Smith did several more scratch tests and finally determined the bracelet was ten karats. He explained he had several testing acids to determine ten karats, twelve karats, fourteen karats, eighteen karats, twenty karats, and twenty-four karats.

"If the gold being tested is the same karat or higher than the acid, the gold scratch will remain, if it is lower, it will disappear. This test is pretty much foolproof, unless you get a crooked broker who's mislabeled his acids. But, if he cares about his reputation, he'll fly the straight and narrow when testing for gold, or he won't be in business for long."

I spent the entire afternoon testing every piece of gold I had purchased from Smith. I bought only small items: rings, bracelets, necklaces, cufflinks, things I could fit in the space beneath my floorboard, and nothing less than fourteen karats of gold. When I finally left the shop with a paper bag of gold clanking in my arms I realized Laszlo would be home from work now and would surely discover what I was carrying. There was no way I could ever explain to him how I had ever gotten the money to purchase so much gold, so I headed to the synagogue.

After the war, Moses Cahn had paid the money out of his own pocket to purchase a new oil furnace for the synagogue to replace the old coal-burning heating system that had been installed by the Odd Fellows back when the building had been their lodge before the turn of the century. The furnace room was low-ceilinged and close, cluttered with stacks of folding chairs used once a year at the High Holidays, mothballed Purim spiel costumes and old prayer books nobody could throw out. If you were not careful you would catch your hair on a nail extending from a wooden beam. In the winter, when the recreation lounge had suddenly gone cold during a gin rummy tournament, I had accompanied Sylvia Rosen down to the basement and the dark furnace room to learn we had run out of oil a day before the monthly oil delivery was scheduled. I was chilled through my wool sweater, so I stepped close to the furnace, which was still hot, and placed my shivering hands close to the boiler, my body warming as heat rolled off in waves. Sylvia Rosen left the door open for me and went to tell the ladies the bad news. As I stood in the dim light, something caught my attention behind the furnace and I carefully made my way through the clutter and cobwebs to discover the enormous coal furnace remained, its black iron shell hunched in the darkness as if in hiding.

Now, I had to crawl on hands and knees with my crinkling paper bag full of gold to reach the coal stove. I felt its clawed feet with my fingers, the decorative sun designs along the side of its iron body, and then found the cool nickel latch on the heavy side door. Evening prayers were going on above me in the small chapel, and I could hear the worshippers chanting Kaddish. I was not like them. I knew for certain their prayers would not find the ears of God, just as I knew God knew nothing of my deceptions. I opened the latch and dipped my hands into the cinders. Piece by piece I placed the gold inside the furnace and closed the door.

Those days were the happiest days of my life, with Laszlo still employed at the watch factory, and me busy almost every day, making deliveries for Moses Cahn, or buying gold from a growing circle of pawn shops reaching from Wallace Avenue as far as Scollay Square in Boston. I learned men would bet on just about anything, from horse racing to dog racing to card games and boxing matches. They bet on baseball and college football and whether it would rain on a Friday and even how much rain would fall. As long as men kept on betting, I continued making my deliveries to the Marino brothers and buying gold.

I only ran into trouble one time after leaving Smith's shop with my parcel of gold, when a man approached me just before dark one winter evening and told me to give it over or else. One of the regulars from The Shebeen happened to be passing by and told the man he didn't want to mess with me; I was with Moe. The man removed his hat, bowed to me, apologized, and went on his way. I was protected by Moses Cahn's brutal invisible hand, more powerful than any protection I ever received from the God of my prayers. People who knew Moses Cahn knew what could happen to them, and it gave me pleasure to imagine the punishment they would receive if they ever tried anything with me.

In the evenings Laszlo and I would go to the pictures or stroll hand in hand along the Charles River. He liked to throw bread to the ducks, and sometimes we sat for hours laughing and talking about our future. He felt he needed to show me the world, but I had seen more of the world than I could handle, and I told him so.

"We can take a cruise to Paris, drink wine on the Champs-Élysées."

"I don't need to travel. Everything I want is right here with me." I grabbed him softly by the ears and kissed him on the lips.

"But you deserve more."

"Laszlo, you need to understand. I already have more than I could have ever imagined. You are all I need."

There were many times I nearly told him about the gold in the furnace. He wanted so badly for me to have material things, to show his love for me to the world. Laszlo was ashamed he could not provide more for me, but I told him I did not need furs and jewels, but he did not believe me.

"What would you do if you had all the money in the world?" I asked Laszlo as a curious duck pecked at the ground nearby.

"I would buy you a mansion," he said, kissing my fingers.

"I don't think I could stand all those empty rooms," I said.

He understood he had opened a door into a dark place, so he pulled me to my feet and said, "Let's dance." He hummed a sweet song softly in my ear, and I let my body sink into his.

Sometimes Laszlo asked me where I had been during the day. He had dropped by the synagogue during his lunch break at the factory and asked the ladies whether they had seen me. Without fail, I told him I had been wandering, wherever my feet had taken me, much like the day the police officer found me screaming by the Charles River. It hurt me to lie to Laszlo like this, and I knew I worried him, but the fact was, once I began working for Moses Cahn, keeping myself busy with a sense of true purpose, building up my collection of gold in case the worst should ever happen again, my aimless wanderings had fallen away.

"There is a doctor in town, a psychologist who specializes in severe trauma. He has been able to help many survivors of the camps," Laszlo said. "I've spoken with him about the fugue state you slip into sometimes."

"I told you, those are finished."

He shook his head sadly, removed his hat and swept his fingers through his beautiful hair. "Sometimes, when we are together in bed, you simply disappear, and I know you've entered some terrible part of your past that is beyond my imagination. You're like a woman possessed, and there is nothing I can do to help you."

"That is not true Laszlo. It is not true. It cannot be true. When I'm with you, my body pressed against yours, I feel safe, truly safe."

He was quiet for a moment, his big blue eyes clouded with tears. "But Fannie, you scream in terror and weep and pound at my chest."

"No," I said. "No. I don't. I don't. I don't."

TECHNICAL KNOCKOUT

Laszlo had been dreaming of buying his own shop since he was a small boy, and since my arrival, Laszlo talked almost daily about making his dream become reality. Now that the watch factory was closing, he saw an opportunity to make a new life for us, in which he would not have to punch a clock anymore and could spend the better part of his days enjoying his time with me. Laszlo had received a small severance package from the factory and had inquired at the bank about a loan.

"The bank manager knew my father and likes my business plan." Laszlo said, rubbing his hands together like a child. "Everybody needs to know what time it is. So everybody needs a watch."

We rushed breathlessly to Levin's Fine Timepieces hand in hand as if we were the only two people in the world. Laszlo was eager to show me around and introduce me to Mr. Levin who had finally decided to sell when the last of his children had passed the bar examination. The front window was jammed with clocks and watches of every type. A sign in the window read: WE DO HOUSE CALLS FOR GRANDFATHER CLOCKS. The entryway was tiled in a black-and-white mosaic of roman numerals surrounding the face of a sundial.

Mr. Levin was a kindly old man who greeted us with a wide smile. A ring of feathery white hair encircled his bald head.

"So wonderful to meet you, Fannie." He kissed my hand with his dry lips. "I can think of no better person to pass my shop on to than Laszlo Schwartz, boy wonder. He used to come in here after school—seven, eight years old—and take apart old watches just to see how they worked. And I let him because he could put them together faster than I ever could. When it comes to the inner workings of a watch, he is the best in the business."

"You're only saying that because Fannie is here."

"Guilty as charged," Mr. Levin said, chuckling. "But there's a shred of truth in every lie."

Laszlo asked Mr. Levin if he could show me the back room.

"You don't have to ask; the shop is as good as yours."

"Close your eyes," Laszlo said. He took my hand in his and led me behind the wristwatch counter and down a narrow passageway that smelled of tools and metal and oil. I could hear the ticking of a thousand clocks. His hand was damp with nerves, and his pulse raced in his wrist.

"All right, Fannie. Open your eyes."

The room was cluttered with watch parts and old broken clocks yet to be fixed. There was a small workbench in the corner and a bright window that showed into the back alley.

"What do you think?"

I did not know what to say, so I remained silent, taking in my surroundings.

"The sewing machine . . . I bought it for you."

Somehow, I had failed to notice a brand-new Singer sewing machine sitting right before me on a wooden table. "It's for you. So we can be together all the time. You can do your tailoring, right here not twenty feet from me. And soon I'll buy you an easy chair so you can knit in comfort."

"I thought you didn't want me to work."

"You won't be working for anyone," Laszlo said. "Just for yourself and for us. You can bring in a few extra dollars with that machine."

Mr. Levin stood in the doorway smiling like a proud parent. Laszlo had planned everything and had not even asked me if this was what I wanted.

"Laszlo," I said. "I'm already very busy. I don't have the time to be here always."

"So you'll miss a few games of bridge with the girls. Isn't this what you want?"

"No," I said. "No. This isn't what I want."

"Aren't you happy for me? For us?"

"Yes, I am happy." As I said the words, I felt like I had fallen down a deep hole. "You can't keep me here. I'm not your prisoner."

"But Fannie, this shop will belong to us."

"I don't care." I rushed out of the shop, leaving behind the mocking ticktock of a thousand clocks.

I'd never seen such a look of heartbreak before, not just on Laszlo's face, but also on poor Mr. Levin's. For a moment, out in the street, I thought of returning and throwing myself in Laszlo's arms, but I could not see that upside down face again, or I knew I would give up everything for him.

I ran. At first, I ran simply to put distance between me and the shop, but soon I realized I was running to Moses Cahn. He was the only one, after all, who had given me the opportunity to be independent, to earn my own money. He was the only one who I wanted to see. I burst into his office. Moses Cahn was on the telephone, chewing an unlit cigar in the corner of his mouth.

"I'll call you back," he said, and hung up the telephone.

My tears had dried, but it was clear from my red nose and glassy eyes I had been crying. He stood up and spread his arms wide. "Come here," he said.

I went to him, and he held me in his brutal arms. His chest was broad, and he smelled different from Laszlo, like a beast of the forest, masculine, powerful and almost wild. He stroked my hair and said, “It’s all right, doll.”

I buried my face in his chest and imagined being locked forever in the back room of the shop, the entire world, the rides on the commuter train, Benvenuto’s pastries and the North End, Beacon Hill, Scollay Square disappearing forever from my life, my legs withering from lack of use. He pulled the blinds closed on the picture window that looked into his shop and the long rows of bottles reaching all the way to the clanging cash register.

“What’s the matter?” he asked.

I said nothing, fearing I would say something about Laszlo I would regret. Moses Cahn poured me a drink and I drank it down in one burning gulp. Already I could feel my muscles loosen and relax. He poured me another. “I remember when you were just a skinny waif, a broomstick in a house dress with a greenhorn accent. But look at you now; you are a woman. I’m glad you stopped by,” he said, returning to his chair behind the desk. I sat across from him and sipped my drink. He told me the fight of the year was going to take place at Yankee Stadium and that the undefeated heavyweight champion Rocky Marciano, would be defending his belt against former champion Ezzard Charles. Three months earlier the *shvartze* went all fifteen rounds with Marciano, but lost on points, the only opponent ever to get that far. I didn’t know anything about boxing. Technical knockouts and points meant nothing to me, but I understood that this fight would involve a lot of money.

“There is going to be heavy betting on the fight,” Moses Cahn said, clutching his glass in his hand. “There’s real excitement, especially around Boston with the Brockton Bomber being a local boy and all. What round will Charles go down? KO or TKO? Some folks are even betting Charles will win. I sincerely doubt that, but the odds promise a big payday." Moses Cahn leaned forward in his seat, "I need to know you are all right carrying all that money. It's a lot of dough and there could be trouble if anyone figures out what you're carrying."

"What are you saying?"

"If you don't think you can make the pickups, I'll send a couple of my men to do it."

"I can do it," I said. "I'm not afraid of anything. I've already seen the worst the world can do to a person."

"You're sure?"

"I'm sure."

"That's my girl," he said. "Let's drink to that."

We knocked our glasses together and drank.

"I'll make sure there's a little extra in this for you."

I knew Moses Cahn had a lot of women because sometimes he would slip me a ten-dollar bill to deliver a trinket or a bouquet of flowers or a box of chocolates to a pale blonde in an apartment on Sycamore Road, or a dark, large-bosomed Sicilian who tossed aside the gift and flashed her teeth at me like a challenge. Over the years, there were so many I lost count, and I wondered whether Moses Cahn's wife knew what was going on behind her back. He poured me a third drink and I had already forgotten why I had been so upset. I felt warm and full of light. I felt pretty as Moses Cahn stared at me, his eyes searching my body.

"What?" I said.

"You are something else, Fannie." He let out a short whistle. "Right here in front of me all this time."

I realized I was drunk and had not eaten anything since breakfast. "I should be going."

"Don't you find me interesting?" Moses Cahn asked.

"Yes," I said.

"Then, what's your hurry?"

"I need to get home to prepare dinner."

"Ah, domestic life." He rocked back in his chair. "You're not like the other broads. Why don't you let me take you out to dinner? You like steak? Sirloin? Filet mignon? I like mine black and blue and bloody as hell."

"Laszlo will be waiting for me."

"That 4-F stiff? Ditch him. You gotta live a little."

I stood and felt myself wobbling, the room teetering around me. "I should be going."

"All right, all right," he said. "Let me drive you. You're in no condition to walk."

He poured himself another glass of scotch, held it to the light and said, "One for the road," and drained his glass.

Moses Cahn was no Clark Gable, but he carried himself with an upright confidence. He prowled rather than walked. Even his finely tailored suits could not entirely civilize him. His dark eyes burned and when he looked in my eyes, his hand pressing the small of my back, I knew he intended to have his way. I should have never gotten in the car with him. But I felt I was attractive around him, sassy, even a little dangerous. Laszlo, in his desire to please me, had made me feel that afternoon like an over-the-hill hausfrau fit only to sew away the rest of her days.

I slid into the front seat of the car and removed a tube of lipstick from my pocketbook. I didn't understand what Moses Cahn would think as I applied the red to my lips, and the Cadillac roared to life.

"Fannie, you really are a genuine beauty," he said turning right onto Wallace Avenue. "Bess Myerson has nothing on you."

"I live the other way."

"What's your hurry? I'll show you the scenic way."

We drove north on the Yankee Division Highway, Moses Cahn silent beneath the drone of the Cadillac's engine. Seeing him in profile behind the steering wheel, I realized his nose was crooked, no longer the sharp straight line I had become accustomed to. I was about to ask him what happened to his nose when I felt his hand on my knee.

"What are you doing?" I asked.

He slid his hand farther up, slipping beneath my dress, squeezing my thigh. "What's the matter, don't you like it?" he said, looking not at me, but at the road in front of him.

"I need to get home," I said. "I'm a married woman."

"And I'm a married man. Looks like we've got something in common."

I pulled away from him, escaping his grip, and Moses Cahn pressed his foot to the gas. Farm fields raced past my window. I could smell the sweet stink of fresh manure, moist in the coming dusk. I rolled the window down and vomited on the outside of the car.

"That should make you feel better," Moses Cahn said.

"Take me home," I said. "Or I will scream."

"I scream, you scream, we all scream for ice cream!" He laughed and pressed his foot to the floor.

We must have been driving eighty miles an hour, weaving in and out of traffic, nearly smashing into the rear bumpers of the cars ahead of us as we passed. The car shook and rattled, and I was afraid it would come apart.

"Slow down. You'll kill us both."

"I thought you weren't afraid of anything."

"I don't want to die."

"And I don't want to kill you. I'll admit it. I'm an old softie. Just promise you'll be nice to me."

"I'm always nice to you."

"I mean now," he said. "If you know what I'm getting at."

"Yes, yes," I said. "Please, please just slow down. Please."

"I can do better than that," he said. Moses Cahn pulled off the highway and into the gravel, rolling to a stop in a grassy ditch. The car sat in deep shadow. The smell of manure was stronger now that we had stopped moving, and I caught a glimpse of myself in the side view mirror. My lipstick was smeared, my hair a mess. Moses Cahn chuckled softly beside me and I felt, now that we were safe, silly for having carried on the way I had.

I turned to apologize to Moses Cahn, and his thick lips met mine. He pushed his sour tongue into my mouth and slid me onto my back across the length of the Cadillac's white leather front bench. He tore open my dress and threw himself on top of me. His unshaven face was rough against mine as he settled himself between my thighs, his knees forcing my legs open.

"No," I said. "Stop." I scratched at his face and drew blood, his skin peeling off beneath my fingernails. For a moment Moses Cahn stared into my eyes. It was the only time he would look into my eyes, and I saw that whatever was human in him had vanished.

"Be nice," he said, wrapping his thick fingers around my throat. "I am used to getting what I want. Don't make me work for it."

He gave a squeeze to my throat, and my windpipe closed beneath his fingers. I let out the most terrible gasp when he loosened his grip, an animalistic moan that sounded nothing like any sound I had ever made.

"Please," I said. "Don't do this."

He removed my underpants and unzipped his trousers. There was a stain on the front of his pants shaped like a map of prewar Poland. I stared at it, wishing myself back into the far past, a time when my body remained mine and mine alone. "Don't be a cold fish," he said. Then he thrust himself into me and I was overcome by the smell of sweat and fresh manure.

It was dark when Moses Cahn dropped me off in front of my apartment. I knew that Laszlo would be worrying, wondering where I was, but I knew there was no way I could let him see me looking like this. Moses Cahn had been quiet after he had done his business, and he drove slowly down the dark side roads until he found his way to Story Street. He was less like himself now than he had ever been, a shadow emptied out of all rage and strength. His eyelids were heavy, and the pink scratches on his face looked wet and raw. He released the steering wheel, let out a long sigh. I stepped out of the car, and into the cooling night, ready to walk away my failings.

I spent all the next day in bed beneath blankets, afraid to show myself to the world. Laszlo called the police when I had not returned home, and an officer found me staring blank-eyed into the dark shop windows on Wallace Avenue sometime after four in the morning.

"This is not right Fannie. I'm worried about you. Will you please agree to see a doctor?"

"Leave me alone, Laszlo. You don't understand."

"But I want to understand. I want to help you."

"Nobody can help me. Just please, leave me alone."

Laszlo was quiet for a long time, but I did not hear his feet move away across the floor. "Fannie," he said. His voice was mournful, full of pain and doubt. "What can I do?"

I wished I could stay forever inside my blanket cocoon, my body curled into itself like a closed fist. I could still feel Moses Cahn inside of me, a burning in the space he had opened up. I could have done more to stop him, but I was stupid and drank too much and allowed his words of flattery to take hold of me. I thought I was different, that he understood what I had been through, and that his brutality could never touch me. But I was wrong.

"Just go to work, Laszlo. I'll survive. I always do."

He stepped closer to the bed, and I could hear him bending over me.

"Don't touch me. Please, Laszlo. Don't touch me."

"Are you angry at me about the shop?" Laszlo said, at last.

"Oh, Laszlo," I said, and began to sob into my pillow.

The fight between Rocky Marciano and Ezzard Charles was postponed for two days because of the weather in New York. I spent that time alone in bed. Rocky Marciano won the fight. He knocked out Ezzard Charles in the eighth round. I heard the neighbors cheering before their television sets and was reminded that the world continued whether I was a part of it or not.

When Laszlo's alarm clock went off Monday morning, I sat up in bed and said, "I love you, and I'm sorry."

He kissed me softly on the mouth, lines of worry furrowing his brow. "You don't need to be sorry. Are you feeling better?"

"Yes, Laszlo, I am."

"Thank God," he said.

"God has nothing to do with it."

I made my first stop at The Shebeen and noticed instantly that the bundle was much larger than it usually was. The regulars were still talking about the fight, about Marciano's tireless right hand, how he wore Charles down with hard blows to his body before finishing him off.

"Six devastating punches and it was all over."

"That's a load of bull," a moonfaced regular with thin, Brylcreemed hair said, barely lifting his face from his drink. "Charles went down in the eighth 'cause the mob told him to."

"You really think a darkie could beat Marciano?"

"In his prime, Joe Louis would've murdered Marciano."

Ordinarily after I made all of my pickups, I would walk over to Walden Station, sit on a bench and wait for the one forty-six inbound to North Station to arrive. Today was different. The bundle I carried in my net shopping bag was heavy, not too heavy for me to carry, but heavy enough for my curiosity to get the better of me. How much money was I actually carrying? I had never counted the money before, as I was expected at Benvenuto's Bakery not a minute after 2:30 p.m. I remembered Moses Cahn mentioning once the number $15,000, and that sounded about right. I imagined I had three times that much in my bag.

It may sound strange to say, but my feet would not carry me anywhere near the station; they turned without my say-so and began marching in the direction of the synagogue. When I arrived, I knew what I had to do. I slipped in the side door so the ladies of the Sisterhood would not be suspicious as I made my way to the basement with such a large bundle. My own regular deposits in the coal furnace were small enough to be contained in my pocketbook, and I covered myself with the excuse that I needed to use the ladies' room.

The furnace room was dark, and I laid my bundles out on the floor before me and lit a match from a matchbox I had taken from The Shebeen. By the time the matchstick burned down to my fingers, I had counted $1,300. I struck a second matchstick and counted again, forming a small pile of bills fanned out around me. When I had exhausted the matchbox, my heart was pounding, my mouth was dry, and I could barely breathe. The sulfurous smell of the matches made me dizzy, and for a moment I was afraid I would pass out in the darkness of the furnace room with $42,370 worth of loose bills scattered around me. I put the money in the furnace, closed the iron door and went to make things right.

Moses Cahn stood up from his swivel chair and spread his arms wide in greeting, "Look what the wind blew in. There's my girl Friday."

I could still feel his horrible body, heavy on mine, his animal grunts echoing in my ears. I wanted to smash his face with my fists, to hurt him in a way he had never been hurt before, but I knew even a thousand blows of my fists would not have the slightest effect on Moses Cahn.

"I'm not your girl."

"Suit yourself," he said and sat back down at his desk. "I'm busy here. What can I do you for?"

"I came to tell you the money is gone."

"What money are you talking about?"

"Rocky Marciano, the fight of the year. The Marino brothers' money. It's gone."

"Gone?" Moses Cahn shook his head in disbelief. "What do you mean 'gone?' What happened?"

"I threw it in the Charles River."

"You've got to be joking."

"The entire $43,000. It sank right to the bottom."

"Why? Why? I'm not even going to ask you why you would do such a brainless thing. Where is it? Where did you dump it?"

"You'll never find it."

"If the Marino brothers don't get that money they will come after me with guns blazing. They will be out for blood."

"I understand that."

"Do you know what those animals did to my kid brother Nathan?" Moses Cahn raked his fingers through his hair. "They shot him right in the face. Nearly took his whole head off. Shot him right in front of his wife and children."

"And yet you still work with them," I said.

"I am biding my time, Fannie. Do you know what that means?"

"I don't care what it means." My words didn't seem like my own but I wasn't afraid that he was going to hurt me. He had already done the worst to me, and if he was going to kill me now, it wouldn't do a thing to hold off the Marino brothers.

He pushed back his swivel chair and stood up. Moses Cahn's face was red, contorted, not unlike his face in the throes of passion. "Close the door."

"If you want the door closed, you can close it yourself. I've said all I have to say."

I turned and walked out of his office and into the liquor store, passing a couple of his men playing cards at the counter. In an instant Moses Cahn was at my back, his breath hot in my ear. "You got yourself into some bad business, baby doll. You're going to pay for this. You know that? You're going to pay, and it's going to hurt more than you could ever imagine."

That night, Moses Cahn knocked at our apartment door. Laszlo was reading the paper in his chair by the window, and I leaped up before he had a chance to move. We were not often visited at home, and it was rather late, but Laszlo did not raise his head from his paper, absorbed as he was with the day's baseball scores.

"Hello, Fannie," Moses Cahn said. He fiddled with a gold ring on his left pinky finger.

I did not respond. He filled the doorway with his terrible form, and I felt him moving inside me. "You must leave. Now."

"I get it," he said. "You want I should pay you some more for your troubles." He removed a billfold from his pocket and peeled off ten one-hundred-dollar bills. He held them out to me and said, "Now where's the money?"

I swatted away his hand. "I'm not one of your shiksa prostitutes. I told you, I threw it in the Charles River."

The expression on his face did not change, but I could see something shift behind his eyes, like the minute hand on a clock moving toward the hour.

"Fannie, where's the money?" He was no longer trying to sound friendly. I heard laughter coming from a television downstairs, *The Burns and Allen Show*. "You've got three seconds to tell me. It's in your apartment, isn't it? Let me guess, under the bed, inside a hat box in your closet. I'll find it."

"I told you I threw it in the Charles River."

"Fan, who's there?" Laszlo called from the sitting room.

"Nobody," I said. "It's nobody."

"Does he know?" Moses Cahn craned his head around me. "Does he know anything?"

I shook my head, wordless.

"This is your last chance to tell me where the money is, or I blow up your whole dream life in this 'golden land.'" Moses Cahn snarled the last part derisively.

"I've gone to the police," I lied. "I've written everything down and told them to open it only if something happens to me or Laszlo. You are a very important man in the community. I understand that a good name is everything. You need to be careful."

"Where's the money?"

"What money?" I hadn't heard Laszlo come up behind me, and now he stood face-to-face with Moses Cahn, separated only by my trembling body. I wanted to close my eyes and open them to a time before I met Moses Cahn, when my biggest concern had been whether or not the people would buy at the sisterhood rummage sale.

"What do you want?" Laszlo stepped between me and Moses Cahn. He was more than half a foot taller than Moses Cahn, but he was slim, narrow-chested with awkward broad shoulders. His ears were red, as if with fever.

"This is between me and Fannie," Moses Cahn said.

"Me and my wife have no secrets."

"Is that so?"

"Listen to me, you crook," Laszlo said. "I know all about you."

"If you know half as much about me as you know about your wife, then you don't know very much."

Laszlo started rolling up his sleeves.

"What are you doing?" I said. I didn't need to hear the answer.

"Let's take this outside," Laszlo said. His voice sounded like something he had heard at the pictures. It was not his voice speaking.

"Sure thing," Moses Cahn said.

Laszlo turned around to kiss me, and I saw in his eyes he had no idea what he was getting into. He did not know what Moses Cahn was capable of. He had not seen him kick the teeth out of the mouth of the mohel, he had not seen Moses Cahn force himself upon me in the front seat of his Cadillac. I held him for a long time around the neck, trying to put off the moment, and whispered, "Don't. Don't go."

"I'll be all right," he said, and he turned away from me right into the hammer fist of Moses Cahn, who hit him right between the eyes.

"Say goodnight, Gracie," Moses Cahn quipped in a fair imitation of George Burns.

"That's a dirty trick," Laszlo said, before he slumped to the floor, unconscious.

"Laszlo!" I bent down to comfort him.

"That's what I call a first-round knockout," Moses Cahn said. "Now, are you going to invite me in?"

Laszlo lay on the floor, his arms and legs bent in strange ways, like a marionette whose strings had been cut. The impression of one of Moses Cahn's rings had left an angry red mark in the middle of Laszlo's forehead. The awful laughter on the TV downstairs filled the air.

"He'll be all right," Moses Cahn said and stepped over Laszlo and into our apartment. "Nice place you've got here."

"Get out," I said. "Or I'll call the police."

"Give me the money, and I'll leave." He sat down in Laszlo's chair and lit a cigar.

"The money is gone," I said. "You'll never get a penny of it."

He blew crooked smoke rings into the air.

"You need to get out now."

"I'll leave when I have the money."

"I told you, it's not here."

"Then you're in a whole world of trouble." He stood up, removed his jacket, and draped it over Laszlo's easy chair. There were large gray stains under his arms. He cracked his knuckles and stretched his neck to the left and to the right.

"Now," he said, "you give me the money, or I take you apart piece by piece."

He stood less than two feet from me, his chest heaving, his breath on fire.

He unsnapped his watch from his wrist and laid it carefully across his jacket. "I'm going to count to ten. I'm going to get the money, Fannie; it don't matter to me if it's the easy way or the hard way. But it sure as hell will matter to you."

I was about to say that he would never hurt a woman, but I knew better. I looked over at Laszlo slumped on the floor and wanted so badly to have a life with just him, a simple life in which Moses Cahn no longer existed.

"Seven. Six. Five . . ."

I had nothing, no money, no strength to fight him off. He would kill me as quickly as he would step on a mouse. I had no choice. I really had no choice. As he finished his counting, he looked me in the eye, a last warning that meant he was all business.

"Say goodbye to those good looks."

He extinguished his cigar into the arm of Laszlo's easy chair, and drew his fist back, three gold rings at the knuckles. Could I survive even one punch from those brutal hands? I never found out. He had taken me once before and I was still alive, breathing in the whiskey on his breath. I knew that if I could just do it one more time, Laszlo and I would have the chance to rid ourselves of him forever, if only he would leave our apartment, somehow I knew we would be all right.

"Stop," I said. My voice trembled. The childish girl in me hoped that Laszlo would rise from his place on the floor and crush Moses Cahn's skull, but it was not to be. Laszlo never had it in him, and that was part of why I loved him so much.

I began to unbutton the front of my dress. My skin was clammy and damp.

"What do you think you're doing?" Moses Cahn asked, with a crooked smile on his face.

"You know what I'm doing."

"So, a little appetizer before the main course."

"There is no money," I said. "This is all I have."

My dress dropped around my ankles, and I stood before him in just my underthings.

"OK, Fannie," he said. "I figured you didn't like it."

I said nothing as he unbuckled his pants and tore off his shirt. "Shall we go to the bed?"

"No," I said, "not the bed."

"All right. The floor is as good as any place." He threw himself on top of me, the stubble on his cheeks tearing at my face like asphalt.

The boy tells me I am one of the lucky ones as he undresses and hangs his uniform neatly over the back of a straight-backed chair. He has brought me a piece of dark chocolate and I snatch it from his hand like it is gold. I know if I fulfill my duties, I will not be hungry tonight and may even live until the end of the war. His skin is pale, and his uncircumcised penis is a terrible thing to behold, like some crawling beast out of prehistory.

"If you will," he says, "Please spread your legs."

He is trying to be kind, and I feel that he is as lost as I am. Kindness cannot exist in such a place as this. We are not alone, and I hear voices behind the thin walls, drunken voices, a laughing eye at the peephole.

"Go get her!"

"The Aryan race loses another virgin."

I see him blush with embarrassment and am filled momentarily with tenderness. He is a boy who does not understand that he will still be a boy when he is finished.

I no longer feel pain when he thrusts himself inside me, even the men who are rough can no longer hurt me. His blue eyes are pale and empty like a young dreamer, lost to himself. I keep my eyes open so that the men know that even if God will not bear witness, I will.

Terrible laughter from behind the partition.

He moves more rapidly now and I know that soon it will all be over, that he will collapse on top of me and dress quickly as if to deny that he has ever been to see me. The cheering rises behind the partition, as he finds his release, and I see in his eyes that he cannot see me as he cries out, "Heil Hitler! Heil Hitler!"

And I begin to cry, not for my own suffering, there are no tears left for that, but for this blue-eyed boy who has lost his way so deeply that when he cries out the name of his beloved, the world dies just a little more.

Moses Cahn screamed out in pain as he rolled off me. The floor was slick with blood, I did not know whose, and he slipped and fell beside me, the rough skin of his face scratched away as if with razors. I realized that I clutched between my fingers two ragged handfuls of hair ripped from the head of Moses Cahn, his scalp, pale white where it had been torn out.

"I can't see," he screamed. "You blinded me."

One of my painted fingernails had broken off in the corner of his eye socket, his eye filled with blood so red it made my teeth hurt. He rolled about the floor screaming in beautiful agony.

I did not know how I had gotten to this place or how I had managed to tear the hair from his head. My shoulders ached where he had beaten me and my jaw stung where his palm had met my cheek, but I had gotten the better of him. He rolled about in pain, pressing his eye back into its place.

"Oh my God, Fannie." I could hear Laszlo rise to his feet and his arms were around me. "What happened?" he shouted at Moses Cahn, "You monster. You'll get the chair for this."

Laszlo rushed to the phone and called an ambulance, giving our address on Story Street. Then he turned to Moses. "I don't know who you think you are, if you ever come near Fannie again, I will kill you."

"Brave words," Moses Cahn said, climbing to his feet, his hand pressed to his shattered eye. "From someone who sat this one out."

"You're finished," Laszlo said. "You'll go to jail."

Moses Cahn laughed and wiped the blood from his face with a striped handkerchief. "Do you think Fannie wants the world to know that I have been fucking her?"

"Liar," Laszlo said.

"Ask your wife."

I shook my head. "We will never speak of this," I said. "And you will never speak to either one of us again."

"Break my heart," Moses Cahn said.

"Get out of my house you dirty dog," Laszlo said, ushering Moses Cahn to the door. "Get out."

Moses Cahn found a cigar in his jacket pocket, struck a match on our doorjamb and lit it. "You're both ruined. I pity you. I really, really do."

Two nights later, Cahn's Superior Liquors burned to the ground, the entire block, fueled by thousands upon thousands of gallons of alcohol, went up in flames, painting the black sky with orange tongues of fire. I had heard Moses Cahn joke about the power of Jewish lightning with the thuggish men in his shop and it was on full display now. I knew that Moses Cahn had burned down his own business so he could pay off his debt to the Marino brothers. But over the coming weeks and months, The Shebeen went up in flames, and so did Jimmy's Barbershop, and a half-dozen other properties that Moses Cahn may or may not have owned. He was through with gambling and was building up his resources for a long winter without a constant flow of cash. That was the beginning of Wallace Avenue's long, slow sickness in which empty storefronts remained unfilled for years at a time. Once busy blocks of shops and businesses now looked bombed-out, boarded up and overrun with angry weeds. It would not be long before the famous Letourneau's Department Store, that drew over ten thousand for its annual Thanksgiving parade along Wallace Avenue, closed its upper floor and began laying off workers, as shoppers moved farther into the suburbs.

Levin's Fine Timepieces survived the fires. I knew it had been spared not as a kindness, but as a punishment, and a reminder that Moses Cahn was not finished with Laszlo and me. The day after Moses Cahn's visit to our apartment, the bank denied Laszlo's loan application with no explanation. Laszlo came to me with stricken eyes, his hands trembling. I knew before the words left his mouth that he would never own his own shop in Walden and that he would have to accept Mr. Levin's offer to run the shop on his behalf at the generous rate of $2.50 an hour. All I could do was embrace him and tell him at least we were together. "As long as you work in that shop, I will never leave your side."

I never once considered using the money I had taken from Moses Cahn to buy the business from Mr. Levin. The money was poisoned. I knew as well, that if I did, Moses Cahn would know I had kept his money and Levin's Fine Timepieces would be reduced to ash with Laszlo and me inside.

We would be together all the time now, Laszlo in the front of the shop, tending to his few customers, and me sewing idly in the back room my burial shroud.

TRUDY'S WEDDING

Trudy Schwartzstein had planned her second and final wedding to be perfect: idyllic beside a shimmering blue pond, almost Gatsby-esque, reminiscent of another, more hopeful era, far enough from the gauzy late summer stink of Manhattan, but not so far away that her 240 guests (excluding a ten-piece soul band, and a surly French chef) would feel obligated to spend their entire Labor Day weekend in the wilderness beyond the Five Boroughs. Trudy had her friend Tammy's forty-acre property at her disposal. She had handpicked variegated seasonal hydrangeas and dahlias on each of the twenty-four tables, name cards written in simple, unadorned calligraphy marking the guests' seats beneath the high vault of the white party tent. She had ordered a dozen cases of Crozes-Hermitage, bottled by Chapoutier, and a dozen cases of Montlouis from the Loire Valley to complement the three-course meal, and an apricot marzipan wedding cake for dessert.

Trudy even had a rabbi who had agreed not to mention God. "Jesus," Trudy thought "that's not even my coup de grâce."

No, the true victory on that day would be the end of Trudy Schwartzstein, the end of that unwieldy last name forever, no more stuttered missteps and tongue-tied tautologies, and no awkward post-feminist hyphens either. Hello world, meet Trudy Sherwood.

ꙮ

It was the hottest day of the year. 102 degrees with 90 percent humidity beneath the burning August sun. The inside of the tent felt like a greenhouse, even with a dozen circular fans stirring the air uselessly. A distant radio played Martha Reeves and the Vandellas, while the catering staff, clad in formal black and white, set up tables with the slow somnolence of lambent sleepwalkers.

Trudy sat in her wedding dress, deflated before a mirror, only an hour before the high-noon wedding.

"I've got an Afro," she said. "I've got a goddamned Afro!"

Her hairdresser, Miri, an Israeli in New York on an expired visa smiled, "More hairspray?"

"Get out," Trudy shouted, thinking: any more hairspray and I'm going to combust.

"This is humiliating," Trudy thought, an Afro on my wedding day, a day she had dreamed about since her divorce, almost ten years earlier. She sat with her head in her hands and consoled herself: Tomorrow, Michael and I will be in Venice.

"Sweetheart," Esther Schwartzstein called entering the bridal tent.

"What is it, Mom?" Trudy said, not looking up.

"The guests are arriving," Esther said stopping short, "Oh, Bunnyrabbit. Is that the way they're wearing their hair in The City now?"

"Don't kvetch to me now, OK? I'm a nervous wreck."

"I'm not kvetching, I'm kvelling. At least you didn't plan some sort of nose-in-the-air art gallery opening with your caviar eggs and squid ink."

Trudy spun on her low stool to face her mother, "You're wearing white!"

"So are you," Esther Schwartzstein shot back.

"Mom, I'm the bride. I can't believe you're doing this on my wedding day."

"Your father and I were married on Labor Day weekend," Esther sighed, oblivious.

"You and Dad are divorced."

"Thank God for that," Esther said. "And I'd divorce him again if I had the chance."

"Wearing white at my wedding is—" Trudy was interrupted before she could say unconscionable.

"I can wear white if I want to. It's still before Labor Day," Esther said smiling broadly at her witticism.

"Why are you torturing me?"

Esther pleaded ignorance.

She looked almost sweet in white and younger than her sixty-three years, still thin, but toned from practicing Ayurvedic yoga, the skin on her face pulled back tightly like cling wrap over a half-eaten Thanksgiving turkey, her dyed platinum hair (somehow!) an immaculate, shining helmet. The dress was understated, even tasteful—and that was what bothered Trudy so much. Her mother wearing white was an act of aggression of which only Trudy would be cognizant. Her mother was sly, and this was payback for Trudy picking out her dress without first consulting her mother.

"You should see what Bobbie is wearing," Esther added referring to Trudy's future mother-in-law. "She looks presentable, except her outfit clashes with her bouquet."

"Bouquet?" Trudy said. "What bouquet?"

"Bobbie's bouquet. The one she's going to carry down the aisle."

Trudy stood up, teetering precariously on one heel, "Bobbie's not walking down the aisle. There's no procession. It's just me and Michael. That's it. Me and Michael forever. We're adults for fuck's sake."

"Do you want me to take care of it?" Esther said.

"Mom."

"Sweetheart," Esther said softly. "My only daughter is getting married—again. I'll do anything I can to make this the most special day of your life. I love you so much. You're my baby." Esther paused and cleared her throat. "Who's the best mother?"

"You are."

Esther smiled, flashing her porcelain-capped teeth, "I'll boot the bitch."

The first guests to arrive were the elderly, conveyed from the distant parking area on balloon-adorned golf carts. Aunt Rennie from Boca Raton, oblivious to the smothering humidity, dressed in a royal-blue suede suit, waved at Trudy calling out, "Hey, gorgeous," as her fourth husband Burt mopped his forehead with a polka-dotted handkerchief. Grandma Dot with her gleaming Trinidadian caregiver arrived wondering when the tournament would begin.

Uncle Israel, Izzy Sherwood, Michael's father's only brother, the putative family patriarch who hadn't spoken to half his family in half a lifetime—including his three no-good sons—arrived alone, resplendent in a blue, double-breasted suit with his signature red carnation hanging limply from his lapel and announced with a skewed approximation of Ed McMahon's bullhorn roar, "Here's Izzy!"

And then under his breath, "It's as hot as a fucking frying pan," as he lit one of his famous cigars.

More family arrived: cousins, uncles, stepchildren—an adopted Asian nephew from Trudy's father's wife's family—all of them slouching toward the shade of the ivory-colored big top.

And then, at the last moment when it seemed it would be only a family affair, they appeared out of the shimmering haze almost magically, materializing in the far reaches of Westchester County as if they had all caught the same ten fifty-five train from Grand Central Station—Trudy and Michael's friends had arrived.

Gary and Lennon, both chorus dancers on Broadway, arrived wearing matching tails and top hats. Michael's boyhood friend, Simon, huffed and puffed up the slope of the grassy hill carrying an outsized gift on his narrow shoulders. Their nonprofit friends came laughing up the hill in vintage clothing, cuffs and sleeves rolled to the knees and elbows, mocking the train conductor's pronunciation of "Scawsdale." They dumped bottles of Pellegrino water on their heads as they reached the crest of the hill and the gray shade of the tent. Michael's All But Dissertation friends from Columbia arrived open-shirted and pale, bewildered by the sun that seemed to be stewing their brains in their shells. Jefferies, the painter, wore shorts and a baseball cap, his jacket coolly slung over his shoulder. Marcus and his Deadhead girlfriend sang "Ob-La-Di, Ob-La-Da," and squirted each other with green neon water guns. Steve, Trudy's former crush from college, arrived last, just in time to see Trudy skipping down the backside of the hill with her shoes in her hands and her dress hiked up to her still-beautiful knees.

Standing beneath the failing shade of an ancient willow tree on the far side of the pond, Trudy felt her butterflies disappear—after all, there was her man. Michael, wearing his third suit of the day, stood with his parents, Bobbie and Max, his two sisters, and his oldest friend, Simon Levy. Uncle Izzy placed a hand on Michael's shoulder and seemed to be giving him a private pep talk before the signing of the marriage contract.

"My man," Trudy thought, smiling.

"Trudy, take off your sunglasses." It was Esther.

Michael drifted over and kissed Trudy on the lips. She noticed that he had a small cut on his cheek, and a dilution of pink blood was running down his neck.

"Mom, the sun is in my eyes."

"Fine. Spoil the photos," Esther said, turning to her ex-husband.

Michael leaned close to Trudy and whispered slowly in her ear, "Tomorrow we'll be in Venice."

"Yes," she said, taking off her glasses and laughing. "Yes!"

Rabbi Judah Greenfield, Michael's boyhood rabbi in Manhattan, his retirement suspended for the day, called the couple to stand before a low table where the ketubah was spread out.

"What happened to your face?" Trudy said.

"I cut it shaving. Three hours ago."

Tall, slim, and white-haired, the revered Rabbi Greenfield called forth the witnesses. Simon Levy stepped forward. And so did Uncle Izzy.

"Neither of you are blood relatives?" Rabbi Greenfield asked.

"Of course, I'm a blood relative, Greenfield," Izzy boomed. "I'm his fucking uncle."

"The ketubah witness must be someone who is not a blood relative," Rabbi Greenfield said evenly, wiping his brow. "The ketubah witness must be someone who has not taken payment, and who has the vested interest of the sanctity of the marriage at heart."

"Here we go," Bobbie said.

"Izzy, go stand next to Max," Trudy said.

"Listen, doll. I love you like a daughter, and Michael like a son—"

"Come on, Iz," Max beckoned, "Forget about it."

"Go take a long shit in your hat, Max."

"I'm not wearing a hat."

"You know what I'm talking about, you simp. I was at the kid's birth, his goddamned bris, his bar mitzvah, and now I'm going to witness this simcha, even if I drop dead."

Trudy could see the veins pulsing on Izzy's neck, sweat pouring from his face. She imagined a gondola on the Grand Canal. Michael put an arm around Izzy, "It was a mistake. We didn't know. But you still get to say the *motzei.*"

"That true, Greenfield?"

The rabbi said nothing.

"Am I still in with the bread?" Izzy asked.

"Give him the bread and let's get on with this," Bobbie said, fanning herself with a wedding program.

It was agreed. Uncle Izzy would say the blessing over the bread. Simon ran up to the house to get Trudy's best friend, Tammy, to stand in as the second witness.

Finally, everybody was ready. Rabbi Greenfield nodded his head at Trudy and Michael and began. "This is an important part of the Jewish life cycle in the eyes of the Jewish people and in the eyes of God . . ."

Through her peripheral vision, Trudy could see Michael's jaw tense at the mention of God

"Continuing the tradition of your ancestors. By signing this ketubah, you are entering into a sacred union before the community and God."

"I can't believe he mentioned God—twice," Michael said, after the signing, and after Izzy had stalked back up the hill, kissing all the women and shaking all the hands.

Michael kissed Trudy and said, "I have to talk to him."

Rabbi Greenfield, looking frail for the first time, withered from the heat said, "Well, Michael." The rabbi offered a handshake and pulled Michael into a warm embrace. "I'm proud of you."

"Rabbi," Michael said, "remember when we spoke after I got engaged and you promised not to mention God at my wedding?"

The rabbi looked surprised and dabbed at the blood on Michael's cheek with a handkerchief.

"I'm a cultural Jew in the humanist tradition," Michael continued.

"Michael, I've known you a long time, through every phase of your life. And the one thing that has been consistent through all the haircuts and girlfriends, trends, and jobs good and bad, is your sense of humor. Please tell me you haven't lost your sense of humor."

"But you promised not to mention God."

Rabbi Greenfield took Michael by the hand and said, "It would even have been OK for you to have worn your African robes. But asking a rabbi to not mention God is like asking a baker to not use dough. God is not going anywhere. I'm going to mention him during the ceremony. He's in all seven blessings, and I'm going to mention him some more as well. So let's get out of this sun and get you married."

After some bargaining, Rabbi Greenfield agreed to say the seven blessings in English, leaving Hebrew, the ancient language, out of all the prayers. Aside from Grandma Dot misplacing the wedding bands with her heart pills and Trudy nearly fainting under the chuppah from the heat, (even her web-thin veil felt as smothering as a blanket) the ceremony was perfect.

Rabbi Greenfield concluded the ceremony by saying, "In these trying times, with evil ascendant, it is more important than ever to continue the traditions of your people." Rabbi Greenfield placed a glass at Michael's feet.

At the signal from Rabbi Greenfield, Michael stomped the glass as hard as he could. The crowd shouted, "Mazel Tov," and they were married.

The guests had some difficulty finding their seats after the ceremony. Trudy had written out the guests' names on a film of rice paper attached to folded card stock and had it arranged on a table by the entrance of the tent but had forgotten to use indelible ink.

"I can't read the cards," one of Esther's friends said, tilting her bifocals down onto the bridge of her nose. "They're blurry."

"I can't read them either," Trudy's former crush, Steve, said.

The carefully written names had expanded in the humidity, bleeding into each other like a shrink's file of Rorschach tests. Jefferies, planted himself at Table One and began wiping the sweat off his bald head with a cloth napkin destined for Trudy's mother. Each member of Michael's family sat at separate tables with their backs turned stubbornly to each other. The band climbed onto the stage and began its sound check, singing the chorus to "Land of 1000 Dances."

"It's a zoo," Trudy said squeezing Michael's hand.

Order was eventually restored, after Michael deputized a half dozen of his friends to seat the guests in a close approximation to what Trudy had planned all those months ago.

Finally, a loaf of challah was wheeled in on a cart and Trudy's friend Tammy appeared at the front of the tent wearing her version of a flapper outfit.

"Is this on?" she said into the microphone.

"Yes!" people called from throughout the tent.

"I apologize for the technical difficulties," Tammy said, laughing awkwardly, her lips muffling against the microphone as she spoke. Trudy waved her to lift the mic farther away from her mouth.

"And now, without further ado, everybody's favorite uncle . . . Izzy!"

There was a smattering of applause throughout the tent. It seemed to Trudy that there were several different parties going on at the same time, and that her and Michael's friends at the back of the tent were more interested in the sprinklers that had just come on to water the verdant grass. Sitting at the small bridal table with her new husband, not far from the glazed challah, Trudy saw Uncle Izzy, his jaw jutting forward proudly like a Mussolini portrait, his silver flat-top, proudly standing at attention, step up to the microphone and offer a curt, "Hullo." He then mumbled the prayer over the bread in his Lower East Side Ashkenazi-accented Hebrew and began to cut the bread with great Grandma Mindel's marble-handled challah knife.

Something's wrong, Trudy thought watching Izzy sawing away at the bread. His eyes rolled back in his head, showing only the whites. He sawed for another second, maybe less, then dropped to the floor, his arm still moving up and down with the blade in his right hand.

Esther's best friend, Rhonda Katz, stood up in her seat and broke a stunned silence, shouting "Oh my God. He's dead!"

A collective gasp rose from the front half of the tent, Trudy and Michael's friends, oblivious, running through the sprinklers outside the tent.

"Somebody call a doctor," Trudy shouted. "What do we do?"

Max Sherwood sat stricken in his seat as his only brother lay on the dance floor, his arm moving mechanically, the knife blade slicing through the air. Izzy's oldest son's wife, Sarah, was a doctor. Izzy hadn't spoken to either of them in almost ten years because of some long-forgotten slight. And there she was, running along the dance floor in her heels, dropping to her knees, and performing artificial resuscitation on the putative family patriarch. Izzy's arm continued to slice up and down as Trudy and Michael and the rest of the family gathered around Izzy's splayed body. Trudy wondered whether Izzy had soiled himself because he stank like dirty laundry.

"Move back," Sarah said. "Give me air."

"What can we do?" Tammy said, her eyeliner staining her cheeks.

"Take him to Valhalla," Sarah answered evenly.

Valhalla, Trudy thought. That's where the souls of dead Vikings go.

"Valhalla Medical Center is a ten-minute drive," Tammy answered.

Trudy ran out of the tent crying hysterically, thinking, "I'm not going to Venice tomorrow. Izzy's dead. He fucked up my wedding. I can't believe I'm not going to Venice."

A moment later, Michael stepped into the sunshine, his eyes as thin as slits, and walked over to Trudy, wrapping her in a tight embrace. "It'll be OK," Michael said. "Izzy's a tough bastard."

But then she saw Izzy being wheeled away in a golf cart, his head hanging limply to the side, the blue and white balloons she had so fastidiously tied onto the back, floating playfully on the thick air.

"We're not going to Venice," she cried.

Michael kissed Trudy on the forehead and said firmly, "We're still going to Venice. Even if he's dead."

"Trudy," Esther Schwartzstein called as she tottered along the grass in her four-inch heels. "Trudy. You're ruining this wedding for everyone. You're out here. Your guests are in there. You're ruining the wedding."

Rabbi Greenfield stepped into the sunshine and waved at the couple, beckoning them to come inside.

"We're staying out here," Trudy called.

Rabbi Greenfield walked over, looked them both in the eye, and put a hand on Michael's shoulder and the other on Trudy's. "Whatever happens today, and some bad stuff has happened, you got married. That's what you take away. That's what happened today."

"Thanks Judah," Michael said.

The band was playing Stevie Wonder's, "A Place in the Sun."

"That's our song," Trudy said.

"Then go on in and dance," Rabbi Greenfield said.

"I'm a disaster," Trudy said.

"Go on."

*

After the meal, the cake was cut, and the music played on. Trudy, shanghaied by her former crush, Steve, danced a slow-dance with him as he said, "Remember the time we—"

But he never got to finish his question because someone reached out and yanked Trudy into a reggae hora, a spinning circle of whirling bodies, sweat pungent in the air, and lifted her onto a chair above the jubilant heads of the crowd, leaving her former crush, Steve behind. Michael was somewhere down below, wearing a pair of bunny ears on his head with his arm around Simon. She could see her father-in-law, Max sacked out in a chair, with a bag of ice pressed to his forehead, an abject look of misery punched into his face and Bobbie laughing obliviously with a friend. She could see her mother in white, posing for pictures, with Rhonda Katz, and Jefferies, his bald head thrown all the way back, drinking wine from the bottle. And then the band was kicking out Parliament's "Up for the Down Stroke," and Aunt Rennie, in her blue-suede outfit was grinding against the lead singer in the most lascivious manner, her neck arched back in ecstasy.

Trudy felt hot all over, her teeth on edge, stomach tight. She felt the presence of the whole wedding party all over her body, within her, through her nerves and veins. Up near the high arch of the tent, where the sun shone brightest, Trudy could see everything down below illuminated in a bright, white light.

"Get me down," Trudy shouted to her friends undulating beneath her. "Get me down. I'm going to throw up."

She found Michael shaking hands with Max's business partners. They stuffed their faces with wedding cake and halvah. Halvah?

Just then Trudy saw Bobbie serving sweating chunks of marble halvah to the guests. "The bride loves halvah," she said. "Loves it."

"I don't love halvah. I hate halvah. I hate everything about halvah."

Bobbie looked hurt, "No. You said you loved halvah."

"No, I didn't.

"Yes. You said at the shower."

"I was being polite."

"Anyway, apricot marzipan. Uch!" And Bobbie went on her way with a tray of sweating halvah raised in the air.

Trudy grabbed Michael by the hand, pulling him away from a man in canary-yellow shirt sleeves. "We're not going to Venice."

"What do you mean?"

"Your only uncle dropped dead at our wedding today," Trudy said. "We're going to a funeral. Like it or not."

ᔕ

A mid-afternoon thundershower did little to kill the humidity—in fact the air was wetter and swampier after the downpour—but it did chase most of the old folks back to their air-conditioning in The City or points beyond. Trudy kissed Max on the forehead and said, "Get some sleep. I'll see you tomorrow." She said goodbye to Grandma Dot, as her caregiver wheeled her away through the muddy grass. Trudy's mother said "Well, you can't help the rain," blowing a kiss to her daughter.

After a round of perfunctory goodbyes, many to people she had never seen before her wedding day, Trudy went back to her bridal tent to take off her stockings. She saw the bandleader snorting a line of coke on her makeup mirror. "It's cool, baby," he said.

"Sorry. Wrong tent." And Trudy backed away.

Michael and Simon raced golf carts up and down the slick lawn, spinning out into turf-shredding donuts in the manicured grass. The remaining guests were covered in mud and Jefferies peeled off his clothes. Others followed, sledding on serving trays down the hill toward the pond.

"Let's go for a swim," Trudy called.

She felt free now, diving into the cool water in her slip, at peace as she dunked her head below the surface, and the noise of the day was blotted out. She saw legs kicking, luminous bubbles, and someone's penis being playfully grabbed. Down she swam to the silty bottom of the pond, her arms stretched before her, the rhythm of her pulsing heart beating in her ears. She felt her hair flowing behind her. Flowing! "I am perfect," she thought, touching bottom.

The band had turned their speakers toward the pond and they were blazing through a horn-heavy rendition of a '70s funk anthem. Trudy found Michael floating on his back, with his eyes closed.

"This has healing powers," she said massaging pond muck into his cheeks and forehead.

"Give me a kiss," he said.

After drying off, Trudy noticed the guests pairing off and wandering up toward the house or the privacy of the woods. The sun was finally sliding down the western sky, flickering its oranges and reds through the trees, lengthening shadows across the trampled grass. A thin silver mist rose almost magically off the lawn, shimmering like diamonds then fading like smoke. "It's beautiful," Trudy thought.

In the distance, she could see a figure stumbling slowly through the grass. "Michael," she said. "Look."

It was Izzy.

Izzy continued tripping his way, zombie-like across the grass until he reached Trudy and Michael. His suit jacket was missing, and his white shirt was open at the neck.

"It's night of the living dead," Trudy said in disbelief.

"You're alive," Michael said.

"You're fucking right I am," Izzy said. "Checked myself out of the hospital."

"We thought you were dead," Trudy said.

"Well, I'm not."

"This is too much, I can't look at him," Trudy thought, her throat clenching. She turned away and was about to shout through her tears, "Get him out of my sight," when she heard Izzy ask, "It's over?"

"Yes," Michael said.

"Aw, I'm sorry, doll. I'm sorry for fucking up your wedding. C'mere."

Trudy heard something plaintive in that gruff voice that she had never heard before. It was clear to her now that nobody had gone to the hospital to check if Izzy was alive or dead.

"Dollface. Mikey," Izzy said in a voice ruined by a hundred thousand cigars. "This was a tough day, and I just want you to know that I'm gonna look out for you, take care of you," he spread his arms expansively, and it was clear he had difficulty lifting his right arm. "I haven't gotten your wedding gift yet. So just name it."

"Izzy, are you sure?" Michael said.

"Sure, I'm sure."

"Our honeymoon in Venice," Trudy said. "You can take care of that."

"That's thousands of dollars," Izzy said, and the words hung in the humid air for a moment like every one of his promises since Trudy had met him, so real and then gone.

"I'm parched," Izzy said. "They pack up the bar yet?"

"No. I don't think so," Trudy said.

"Help me up the hill then."

Trudy gave Izzy her hand, and they slowly climbed the hill.

WHEN THE RAINS CAME

At first, we did not see the rain fall from the sky, though we did feel the damp in the air, in the steel of our bones. The still sky was gray, the gray clouds full of flood, saved up and timed as though to wash our sins from earth all at once. The rain fell for four long weeks with no pause.

"This is no good," Hank Struck said, as he made the sign of the cross and sank down in the dark muck that took his front porch, his red four by four and his pet black lab. We lost a lot of good men, drowned by the roll of the waves on our own main street. Sharks and rays and a big blue whale made it known they were here to stay. They stove in our homes, knocked the walls in, smashed doors to pieces, pushed us from our beds, ate our wives, stung us, bit us, sent us out to face our fates.

Those of us still left met at the church at the top of the hill. We climbed to the wood pews that bobbed up and down, high up, by the stained-glass saints. The priest said, "God has left us."

"Why? What did we do wrong?" we cried.

"I don't know," the priest said. "But if you have faith, you will know that we have sinned and that we will die for our sins."

A shout went up from a sleek black-haired boy not more than nine, who told us that he had not sinned. He was young and free of guilt in this world. "I have gone to school. I have played games in the woods and in the street and have been fair to my friends. I have read good books, and I have done my chores. I have done no wrong."

"We have all sinned," the priest said with fire on his breath. "And now we are to die."

The boy, sure of his words, stripped off his shirt and showed us all that he had grown gills at his chest and neck, webs at his hands and feet, a sharp fin at his back. And with that, he dove from the pew into the depths of the church and swam out to meet the day. Then, one by one, the boys and girls of our town plunged past him like a school of fish in search of the light.

EMAILS FROM MY DEAD MOTHER

They started a month ago, the emails, always urgent, always comically misspelled, selling bargain hard-on pills, knockoff Rolexes, cheap Canadian meds, and miracle diet secrets insisting I "CLICK THIS LINK!" Normally they would have gone right into my spam box, or if they slipped through, as they can, I would've erased them without thought. The difference this time was the emails were sent from my mother's Gmail account, and she's been dead over two years.

Some sick fuck in Moscow or Vladivostok must have hacked into her email and was using her address as a springboard for some shady black-market commerce. I normally wouldn't have responded—it's become easy to disregard anything that smacks of scamming, and these emails were scammy to the max. But there was something so wrong about this. I'd just visited my mother's grave three weeks earlier and found it impossible not to imagine her lonely, denuded bones laying still in the cold darkness beneath my feet.

I clicked reply, mustered all my righteous indignation, and began to type:

> Listen up, Igor,
>
> You twisted, motherless fuck, I find this whole practice of stealing people's emails for your nefarious purposes to be repellent, repulsive, and utterly despicable, particularly since you are using my late mother's email for your schemes. I call on all of my superpowers for you to get cancer of the eyeballs and die alone on a freezing Moscow street, ignored by everyone but a pack of wandering wolf dogs who piss on your steaming corpse before you are butchered by a dyslexic orphan and sold as prison grub to some hellhole gulag in outer Siberia. I'm sure you have not read Dead Souls by Gogol—you might want to take a look. Go fuck yourself, you scumsucking cunt.
>
> Sincerely, Elmer J. Fudd

I was surprised how my heart raced as if I had just run up four flights of stairs. I was sweating and was pretty sure I was about to cry when a response arrived in my inbox. I opened it and read:

> You always did have a terrible temper, Rooster. Remember the time you kicked your clogs through the glass door?

No one else, aside from my father, knew I'd been called Rooster, due to the unlikely shock of red hair I had until I was six months old and partly as a result of the gravelly way I cleared my throat as an infant—I sounded like a sick rooster trying to crow. I spun in my swivel chair and thought, "What the fuck?"

Back in third grade, I did kick a wooden clog through a frosted glass door in my apartment complex after my mom had sent me to apologize to a friend for stealing one of his plastic army men. Humiliation piled on top of humiliation—he'd stolen worse from me and never apologized. And there I was in those ridiculous clogs she made me wear for some reason known only to her, and I just kicked my foot out of frustration, embarrassment, and off it flew through the safety glass, shattering it like diamonds all over the terrazzo floor.

But my mother is dead, and everything she ever knew, good and bad disappeared with her. Nobody else could know the details of what that person had just written.

A chat window popped up.

> You still there?

I quickly typed in:

> I didn't know hell had the internet.

An answer appeared right away:

> "*Velly* funny," the Chinaman said.

It was her, all right.

You got a tattoo.

I asked her, like an idiot still looking for approval, if she liked it. The names of her two grandsons were inked onto my forearm with thick black lines.

> You know how I feel about hearts. You could remember me with a tattoo on your chest with "Mom" in the middle. It'll look lovely when you finally build up some muscle.

I turned off my computer, poured myself two fingers of shitty potato vodka and drank it straight up, no chaser. Dead, and still a passive-aggressive narcissist. Was I losing my mind? I thought about calling my wife at work, but she never liked my mom and didn't like talking about her, and anyway, she would've told me to call my shrink. Three drinks down and feeling emboldened, I booted up the computer to see if shutting it down had gotten rid of her. Right away, a message appeared on the screen.

> You had a lap dance from some Brazilianed, bump-and-grinder at the Silver Slipper.

Now, I was terrified. Did she know everything I did? Did she know how much I was masturbating these days, and who I was thinking about when I did so? I felt like I needed a shower, but the thought of getting naked in front of my mother gave me the heebie-jeebies.

The next time I looked at the screen, the words, YOU NEVER VISIT appeared in obstinate all caps.

Even from beyond the grave she had the power to enrage me, and I punched the drywall above my desk. The month before I'd driven nine hours to visit her grave, and here she was complaining.

"You're dead," I wrote.

> And still, you never visit.

I typed faster than my fingers would let me, explaining how it was not easy for a father of two young boys, busy with a full-time job to just pick up and drive four hundred miles to stand for five minutes over a desolate gravestone.

> So why only five minutes?

I did the respectful thing. I went to her grave, swept some stray leaves off the stone, plucked a few weeds, and wondered fancifully about the people she was buried beside. Was she in a good neighborhood with the right kind of people? Doctors, lawyers, and the like? Was there pleasant sunlight? Birds singing pretty birdsongs in the trees nearby?

I've never understood what people are supposed to do when they visit the dead. I've never been the praying type; it just seems like talking to yourself, and once you start talking to yourself, it's a slippery slope, and before you know it you're rubbing shit in your hair and calling it gold.

"Let's meet for lunch," she said.

> That's possible?

> You have to eat. How about Scaramouche?
> The crispy duck spring rolls are to die for.
> And the view is spectacular.

My mother was always hustling something. Whether she was borrowing a soon-to-be former-friend's Mercedes-Benz, or scamming a free night at the Waldorf Astoria, where she wasn't even staying, because she found a condom under the bed, or digging up distant relatives who would take pity on her and lend her a couple grand to get her things out of storage. I knew she would claim there was no money in the afterlife, so lunch would be on me. I knew all her tricks, and had, with great shame, integrated some of them into my own life. I knew she would order the ten ounce filet mignon, or if it was on the menu, the lobster, or maybe both. She would drink two Chopin dirty martinis with three skewered olives, and order dessert, always dessert. Then glassy-eyed and imperious, she would abuse the waitstaff for misunderstanding her sophisticated needs. She would leave with a steaming tinfoil of leftovers in her purse, intended from the very moment of ordering to extend the bounty another day. There was no getting away from it—if I met her for lunch, it was going to cost me.

Meet me in an hour?

An hour? That's a long drive.

Maybe I'll just come to you.

I didn't know what to tell my wife. She knew better than anyone my mother had a pathological habit of overstaying her welcome. My mother could be delightful, funny, even charming for an hour or two, but once she laid out her scented candles and toiletries on the bathroom counter, she was *home*, and it would take more energy than I could possibly muster to get her out. She had been evicted from every apartment she lived in after I left for college, and those evictions were bitter, slow-motion affairs that were Pyrrhic victories at best, by the time the exhausted landlord had her permanently removed.

I picked the dirty clothes up off my bedroom floor and tossed the comforter over the bed. The bathroom smelled of pee where the boys had overshot while crossing swords, so I got down on my knees and scrubbed until my elbow hurt. This was crazy; I was cleaning up for a dead woman.

When it came to my mother, I had done more than my share of cleaning—my wife and I both had. When she had died, alone in her one-bedroom luxury apartment, not a penny in the bank and no income to speak of, we had been summoned by the super to clean up the mess she had left behind. The coroner had taken the body; thankfully I was not expected to identify it. The apartment was stuffed with every useless knickknack she had ever come into contact with, every birthday card she ever received, and—God—even my old report cards from elementary school when I was still a clueless dork with buckteeth and a Jewfro and barely knew what planet I was on. She had clothing, mounds of it, not just her own, but vintage back-in-style-again clothing of friends and family members who had predeceased her. It took us four full days to clean the apartment down to the bare parquet floor, the sour stink of death never for a second leaving my nose.

"Fuck you," I said to no one, and like my two boys, I pissed on my bathroom floor. I had no intention of cleaning it up.

I didn't know what to expect. Would she arrive as she had looked in life, done up in designer clothes she couldn't afford, her hair all brassed like a politician's wife, or like the wasted husk she had been before she died, a frosted fright wig slipping from her scalp? She probably wouldn't bother ringing the buzzer like a normal person, that much I could count on.

While I waited, I sifted through old photo albums she had kept of me as a child. There she was, so young, feeding me a bottle of baby formula, my tiny eyes closed, a soft, blue, giraffe-stitched blanket swaddling me tight. My mother and me riding a white folding bicycle, me, bald and clueless, my mother smiling a bright, effortless smile. There we were in the snow, tobogganing down a short hill, her arms thrown around me, and later, in Italy, before the Duomo di Milano, my mother pretending she was my older sister so the man she had just met behind the camera would treat her like a prospect and not some worn out suburban divorcée looking to get her yeah-yeahs out with the local color.

I found another album documenting the early years of her courtship with my father, a time when she blazed so brightly with the arrogance of youth that the very idea of dying seemed an impossibility, the word cancer, not a sentence but a harmless, abstract noun.

There she was on her wedding day, dressed in white like the virgin she was, looking directly into the camera, an easy smile on her face, challenging the future: I am ready for you.

And the amazing thing was, looking at that narrow face, her olive skin and thick dark hair, I realized for the first time, really understood, that she and I looked exactly alike at that age. As the sun began to shift, and long shadows fell across my living room carpet, I thought it would be nice to see my mother again.

Lunch time was long past, and my stomach protested my neglect with a few sour gurglings. I put the photo albums back in their place and went to my computer.

There was an email from my mother.
I opened it and it read:

> hEllo dearest darling. I am barrister lawyer Philip Babangida and I represnet the lately diseased prince Ado Egbule. My esteem client and his Wife and 2 children perish in plane crash bound for your home city. The bank issued me a notice You have been named sole benefactor of his fortune £100,000,000! All I require is your honest cooperation from you and strict confidentiality. I very much look forward to a speedy response from you. Kindest regards Philip Babangida.

BIAFRAN MAN

That summer, the boys of Owl Bunk called the new kid who never spoke "Polio Arms," "Mr. Skin and Bones," and sometimes, when feeling particularly cruel, they called him "Biafran Man." Most of the kids at Camp Elk Horn knew each other from their privileged lives back in the city and the elite neighborhoods and suburbs of Westchester County in which their parents themselves had been raised—from middle school and Sunday school, weekend soccer games and track meets, to Saks Fifth Avenue and Barneys where they bought brand-name everything without a second thought of expense. They shipped out for the wilderness for eight weeks every summer and returned to their parents tanned, healthy, and full of a youthful, loudmouthed bravado that is often mistaken for self-confidence.

They didn't know the skinny kid with big teeth and all the wrong clothes who came on financial scholarship—a foster kid out for his first summer at camp. They'd never seen anything like him before. He was short for his age, starved looking, with pale chopstick legs, protruding belly, and prominent ribs pressed hard against his child-sized Mets T-shirt. His ears seemed too big for his head, sticking out awkwardly like vestigial wings. That first day, he sat quietly on his unmade bunk, deflated duffel bag at his feet as Jordan Davis asked him his name, not unkindly, so I'm told. The dark-eyed boy did not even look up, absorbed as he was in some internal dreamscape unfathomable to the hormone-high thirteen-year-old boys of Owl Bunk.

"You're not going to tell us your name?" he said in disbelief.

The boy said nothing.

"Well, it looks like we'll have to give you a name ourselves."

You can still see the graffiti nearly thirty years later, high up under the rafters where they stored their sleeping bags and mess kits, behind the iron frames of their bunk beds, scratched into the soft pine walls: "Eat Shit, Biafran Man," "B.M. Hungry for Cock!" "Skin and Bones Club: Members, One."

It was my second summer working at Camp Elk Horn and my first as counselor of the boys of Owl Bunk. I had never gone to camp as a child, and I was entering my senior year at Hunter College in Manhattan. I shared a tiny roach-filled apartment with my two pothead roommates deep in outer Brooklyn near the end of the L line, far beyond the reach of even the most intrepid would-be artists and dreamers. The prospect of spending two months upstate in the wilds of Orange County thrilled me, gave me hope that the future was full of camaraderie and togetherness, rather than the brutish poverty of takeout pizza, one-night stands, and hangovers, a spiritual and financial condition I expected to change little after I graduated the following year with a degree in English literature and no real job skills or prospects.

Over the years there had been stories that had become part of camp lore, the poor kid who wasted away to nothing and simply vanished. Counselors before me had been known to warn their younger campers if they didn't clean their plates, they would disappear the same way that boy did. But I never went in for that kind of talk, believed it to be in poor taste. I came to camp to have fun, clean fun, not to inflict psychological damage on my juniors.

The strange thing about the boy was, at mealtime, even among the cat calling and cajoling of his bunk mates, he ate like a lumberjack: six grilled cheese sandwiches and a greasy haystack of fries in a sitting; another time he scarfed down three servings of pancakes before the counselor had finished his own towering pile; then there were the three foot longs fully dressed, and the countless servings of spaghetti, oatmeal, and ordinary cold cereal; he even put away terrifying amounts of tuna casserole, a delicacy the rest of the cabin gladly skipped. He ate like he had never eaten before, and he looked the part. For their first Sunday night snack, after campfire, it's been said, he devoured eight PB&J sandwiches and four glasses of milk. He seemed intrinsically to know when they had messed with his food and slipped Ex-Lax into his chocolate milk or mopped the toilet bowl with his hamburger bun, and he simply looked past it like it wasn't even there. With all that eating, he never gained any weight. In fact, as the first week rolled into the second, he seemed to be losing weight, barely a pale erasure on the distant horizon of the heat-drenched soccer field.

At swim class, they laughed at the captain of the Starvation Army as his desperate head bobbed on the water like an inflatable buoy; at archery, they drew crude pictures of his face and pinned it to the target; and when Andrew Marks yanked down his Lee jeans flood pants before Blue Jay Bunk, exposing his shriveled hairless penis to the fifteen-year-old girls laughing in their bras and panties, he took it all with stoic resignation. He never cried, never spoke a word of protest as they tortured him with hard-knuckled noogies, towel snaps, atomic wedgies, pink bellies, and cruel, nipple-twisting purple nurples.

The annual Sadie Hawkins dance was still a mandatory event then, and the counselors made sure every boy and girl attended whether they wanted to or not. He appeared among the happy, dancing teens and preteens in a checked short-sleeved shirt and a mismatched bowtie and patched-at-the-knees corduroy pants which showed several inches of striped, white sweat socks above his battered black shoes. He sat in the dark on the hardwood bench, his feet barely touching the floor. Three or four songs in, a sympathetic counselor-in-training, a yellow-haired girl named Mandy with enormous breasts and silken hair plaited into thick braids asked him to dance. It had to be a joke—it had to be. All the boys worshipped Mandy and a bounty had been out all summer for the first boy who snatched a pair of Mandy's satin panties.

He barely came up to her shoulders. But as the boys of Owl Bunk looked on, they realized it was no joke at all. He could dance! He spun and twirled and moved about the floor with the ease of a river trout. He and Mandy danced the Time Warp, with a jump to the left, and a step to the right. He thrust his pelvis, and she laughed and held him by those narrow hips, puffing out her red lips like the freakish Dr. Frank-N-Furter. At the end of the dance, she gave him a long hug and he smiled—he actually smiled. It drove the boys of Owl Bunk insane.

Back in their cabin, the boys, pumped full of testosterone and pent-up sexual aggression agreed it was a good time for a game of come on the cookie. Each of the nine boys sat on the floor in a circle around a chocolate chip cookie someone had grabbed at dinner. The premise was simple: they would all masturbate and relieve themselves onto the cookie, the last unfortunate boy to empty his load would have to eat it.

They began with a solemn statement about their words being their bond and the importance of keeping one's promise. Then they each vowed if they were the last to finish, they would eat the cookie—crumbs, come, and all. Someone dimmed the lights, jury rigging a tarp under the fly-spattered light bulbs, providing a greater sense of occasion. Jordan Davis whipped his out and began chanting "Man-dee, Man-dee, Man-dee!" He was the de facto leader as he already had a full pubic beard and claimed to have gone down on Courtney Strathers the first night of camp. The boys removed what they had with varying degrees of confidence and began beating away to the continuous chant of "Man-dee, Man-dee, Man-dee!"

That was when he arrived, late from the dance after disappearing God knows where, to the sight of nine thirteen-year-old boys, eyes clenched shut, fully in hand. He wore a new braided yellow and blue lanyard bracelet at his wrist. It was David Green who noticed him first, and distracted in his frantic stroking said, "What are you looking at, faggot?" The boy stood frozen in the doorway, afraid to enter and afraid to run. Lights out was in ten minutes and the counselors were smoking illicitly nearby beneath the stand of pines.

Jordan Davis, without missing a beat said, "You'd better hurry up and get started or you're eating this cookie."

It would have been hard to tell if he blushed or blanched in that dim light, especially seen through the lens of impending ecstasy, but it would have been clear he had no intention of taking part. He showered in his bathing suit like a shy nine-year-old and dressed in the bathroom after the rest of the cabin had slipped out for breakfast.

"Oh baby, I'm coming," Jordan Davis said as he tumbled like a rag doll on top of the chocolate chip cookie. A second, third, and fourth boy followed, sliding on their knees through the pearly ejaculate as they made their contributions.

When they were all done their business, you might have thought they would have been mellowed by the sweet release of their vital fluids onto the cookie, the object of their adolescent endeavors satisfied. Still, the thin boy stood there in the doorframe as the brief afterglow was replaced by shame and pride and a half-dozen unnamed emotions.

"Looks like you've got to eat it," one of the boys said, snapping the elastic waistband of his Adidas soccer shorts back into place.

"Yeah, he'll eat anything."

He didn't run or approach the boys—he stayed right where he stood and seemed to try and shrink away to nothing, to dematerialize, as a half-dozen rough hands grabbed him and pushed him face first into the floor. One of the boys tried to yank off his lanyard bracelet, but he tucked his wrist protectively into his armpit as they pushed him closer to the cookie.

"Eat it," Jordan Davis said, "Eat it or die."

Someone kicked him and another punched him in the kidney, and he fell forward, his bony ass in the air. Someone called out for a broomstick and said if he didn't eat the cookie, he was getting corn-holed tonight.

"We're being fair," Jordan Davis said, laughing sadistically. "You've got a choice, the cookie or the cornhole."

He shook his head rapidly side to side, signaling no, no, no.

When Andrew Marks appeared with the broomstick, a glob of hot cinnamon toothpaste smeared on the tip, the boy cried out one single word, the only word any of the boys that summer could recall him saying: "Why?"

Then he gathered up the cookie in his trembling hands and began, piece by soggy piece to eat.

"He's eating it! I can't believe he's eating it! That's totally sick," one of the boys said, hyperventilating beneath his laughter.

"What would Mandy think of this?"

"Someone get a camera. Quick!"

When he had finished every crumb, exceeding nearly everyone's most morbid expectations, he stood up and spread his pipe cleaner arms wide to show he had completed the task. His eyes were blank and his mouth a pink blur. And then his little face crumbled, and he threw up everything onto the floor.

In the still silence that followed there was still a chance to show him compassion, humanity—all someone had to do was step forward and hustle him off to the bathroom to clean him up, offer him some Listerine and a few kind words for following through on this terrible enterprise. But the fresh, sour vomit writhing on the cabin floor was an affront to Jordan Davis's idea of right and wrong, and he nudged the boy forward and said: "You know you've got to eat that."

Nobody in Owl Bunk had ever seen anyone run so fast before, bursting out the screen door like a flash of afternoon sun through a thick stand of trees, he was gone. Without a trace. No one saw him running down the gravel path past the boys' cabins toward the lake or the dark of the forest. The night watchman saw no one hotfooting it for the main road. He wasn't hiding behind the girls' damp towels strung on taut laundry lines or huddled in the dirt by the lakeshore beneath a capsized canoe, he wasn't up a tree, clinging, clinging, and he wasn't tucked away beneath a dining table and the protective curtain of the slick ketchup-stained oilcloth.

He was just gone. His disappearance gave new meaning to the saying "disappeared into thin air," and the boys of Owl Bunk joked, before the heavy hand of discipline came down, that he had vanished into the thinnest of thin air. The police dragged the lake and found no body. Search parties canvassed the area for a long time afterward, scoured the forest for miles around and found no sign of the boy, no footsteps, no tracks, nothing. Even a platoon of freshman West Point cadets invited up from Garrison early that fall to run their orienteering drills came up empty. He was simply gone.

All those years later the walls had never been whitewashed, the iron-framed bunks remained the same. Boys still came and went and slept beneath the same roof where that boy had suffered. The incident had hardened into something resembling myth more than reality, as most of the campers took the story to be apocryphal anyway. Time has a way of dulling horror to the point at which fact seems more a fiction or fable. But every time I crossed the threshold into Owl Bunk, I felt a great sadness fill me, knowing that if he were still alive today, he would be twice my age.

My summer was going well, the boys of Owl Bunk were age appropriate in their antics and habits, and I was starting to see a girl I liked named Cathy, who was a counselor for the girls of Robin Bunk. I felt competent for the first time in a long time, and I felt confident about the possibility of future success in an adult world.

One afternoon during a nature walk out in the woods with my boys—and by this point of the summer, some four weeks in, I did feel a sense of ownership over them, even kinship, Jason Rose, a tall athletic kid from Scarsdale, appeared before me, banging what I thought was a pair of drumsticks on the side of the tree. Several of the boys had brought drumsticks that summer and clacked them incessantly on tables, floors, walls—would-be Keith Moons or John Bonhams cutting their teeth all summer long. He pounded out a relentless rhythm, chanting what he thought sounded like an ancient Indian spiritual.

I realized though, aside from his Nalgene bottle, that he had entered the woods empty-handed. I didn't want my boys littering the pristine floor of the forest with their comic books and candy wrappers, so I always made sure to check before we headed out that no one was carrying anything they might leave in the woods. I asked Jason where he got the sticks and he said, "Over there. In the ditch."

Three or four boys stood at the foot of a giant pine tree, staring down at something I could not see. As I approached, I heard one of the boys ask, "You think it's human?"

"Naw, probably a bear cub or something."

As soon as I saw the bones, curled in a bed of dry leaves in what looked like a fetal position, I knew it was that poor boy, clutching his scrawny knees to his chest for close to thirty years. He looked so small, like a child in second or third grade. Tiny shreds of clothing were still fused to the bone in places. And the lanyard bracelet Mandy told the newspapers she had given him that night after the Sadie Hawkins dance, he was still wearing it. I didn't want to alarm my boys, but I felt a surge of panic rise in my throat. This boy had died alone in the woods and had never even been given a proper burial. How could it be that nobody ever found him until now?

"Don't move," I told the boys, deputizing Andy Sears who had just celebrated his fourteenth birthday and had a mangy scribble of mustache on his upper lip. "I'll be right back. Just don't touch anything."

I ran as fast as I could to the Program Director's office and found him sipping a cup of coffee behind his desk. I told him what I found, and he said, "Jesus Christ. After all this time, this is the last thing we need."

The program director was a veteran of over forty summers at Camp Elk Horn, first as a camper, then as a counselor-in-training, then counselor, head of sailing, section head and for the last three summers serving in his current position as PD. His attorney's brain contained the entire institutional memory of Camp Elk Horn, and he could easily recall the bad times as well as the good. He knew by heart the names and home phone numbers of camp's biggest donors and planned to be buried at the foot of the camp flagpole when he died. He wore his salt-and-pepper hair short and dark Ray-Bans dangled from blue Croakies around his neck. "What exactly do you want me to do?"

"I think the child at least deserves a decent burial."

"He's not a child," the program director said. "He's not anything at all anymore. Listen, he has no family to speak of, he's barely a memory. Why do we want to bring back all that pain and heartache just to move some bones from one place to another?"

"Because it's the right thing to do."

A window fan whirred, filling the momentary silence as the program director searched for the right words. A strip of flypaper dangling above his head quivered.

"Do you know how much enrollment dropped after that poor boy died? Trust me I was as horrified as anybody, but that was a long time ago, a generation ago. More, even. It took nearly ten years to get enrollment back up to where it was before the incident, and I'm not about to remind the world that one of our campers died while under our care."

"You can't just leave his bones out there," I said.

"You're right," he said after a moment. "We'll gather them up and put them away somewhere."

"Just *put them away*?" I said. "Where? In a storage closet somewhere with the old softball pennants and sailing trophies?"

"What do you want? A memorial, a benefit concert? This is ancient history." The program director stood up, pushed his chair back and slipped on his Ray-Bans. "Show me where."

When we returned to the woods, the boys were going crazy, running here and there chasing each other with upraised bones in their hands, whooping and hollering with the kind of boundless joy that is unique to the very young. Wolf Bunk had joined them in their merrymaking and howled through the woods clattering slim leg and arm bones like swords. Wolf Bunk's counselor Robbie, an illicit marijuana smoker, was nowhere to be seen and Andy Sears stood guard helplessly over the remains of the remains. He was crying. "I tried, I tried, but I couldn't stop them." He cradled something in his muscled arms and handed it to me. It was the boy's skull. I looked at the empty eye sockets and comprehended the enormity of what I held in my hands. A person, a real human being had looked out on a harsh world through these darkened holes, a young person just starting out who did not survive his childhood and was mourned by no one.

The program director grabbed the skull from me and removed a bright silver whistle from his shorts pocket. He slipped it in his mouth and blew it in sharp repetitive blasts until the forest went silent.

"No one is leaving this forest until all those bones are in this garbage bag." He shouted in his most stern director voice. He produced a black Hefty bag from his back pocket and shook it out.

I'd guess that fewer than half the bones were ever returned, as some were tossed amid horseplay and laughter deeper into the woods, into the quick running stream, up into the dense foliage of the tall trees, or were simply broken to dust beneath the furious hammering of mindless youth. Some of the smaller bones, tiny ring-like vertebrae, finger bones, toes, I imagine were hidden away in underwear waistbands as keepsakes, good luck charms, war booty to show off to disbelieving friends back in the city. This was, for all of them, their first true contact with death, and they had triumphed, at least for now. I found the yellow and blue braided lanyard bracelet curled among some dry leaves and, without thinking, slipped it into my pocket. I saw no purpose in hiding away the bracelet with the rest of his remains. Even after all this time, its bright color had not faded, the knots pulled tight and firm, a symbol of something meant to last forever.

The program director was satisfied with the heft of the black trash bag, but I knew the boy was still out there scattered, alone, disrespected even now. The boys of Owl Bunk and Wolf Bunk were made to swear on their honor they would never tell a soul what they found in the woods. Punishment for the slightest transgression was immediate expulsion from the camp and blacklisted from any future camp events. The boys were silent, solemn as they nodded their heads in assent. But I saw them pulling faces and laughing when the program director's back was turned.

I just wanted to say one thing to them, not to scare them or shame them, just to make them understand that life is precious, and we all deserve to be honored in our death, but the program director forbade me from speaking, prohibited me from saying these few simple words: "Imagine if this was you."

August began with a terrible heat wave, with oppressive humidity blanketing everything as temperatures hit the mid-nineties. My boys wandered listlessly from swim instruction to arts and crafts that first morning, heads lowered, faces blank. It was the heat, I was sure, as there was no air-conditioning at the camp, and the two floor fans brought in to the cabin in anticipation the night before did little but stir the hot air from one place to another. I told my boys they each needed to drink an entire bottle of water every hour and to keep themselves cool by not exerting themselves too much. I went to the rec hall and gathered up some board games and playing cards, hoping they would keep themselves busy until they regained their energy.

By late afternoon, the entirety of Owl Bunk lay sacked out on their beds, not quite asleep, but not quite awake. Some of the boys, heads lolling limply to the sides, drooled, or ground their teeth ferociously. I was frightened by what I saw and checked in on the boys next door at Wolf Bunk. Robbie sat, head in hands, in a broken-down Adirondack chair on the front porch of the boys' cabin.

"They've just been walking around the cabin repetitively in these sort-of-creepy patterns, like they have been programmed by some maniac."

The first thing I noticed upon entering their cabin was that the entire place smelled like rotting meat. The boys who were not laid out on their bunks moved about in twitchy, nervous patterns, their faces empty of their usual vitality. After a moment, one boy broke off from his routine, and I followed him into the back of the cabin where the sinks and toilets were situated. He knelt before the toilet bowl, lapping up the filthy water with his black distended tongue, his body trembling as he did so.

I probably should have gone to the nurse first thing that morning, but in my naivety of all things medical, I was certain it would pass. I was certain now it would not simply go away. The nurse practitioner arrived at Owl Bunk in a flat-out run, cell phone pressed to her ear. "These boys must be quarantined at once," she said breathlessly.

"What's the matter with them?" I asked.

"I don't know."

Their parents were called and told not to panic as they were apprised of the situation. Some of the parents wanted to pick up the boys immediately, but the overwhelmed camp secretary said it would be too risky until it was determined how contagious the condition was. Indignant voices were raised, and lawsuits were threatened, but what could they really do? This was a medical crisis of unprecedented scale. The program director too had taken to his bed and the various section heads ordered the rest of the camp to stay within five hundred yards of the boys' cabins until further notice.

The nurse practitioner established that the causative agent was either a bacteria or a virus, which meant that the boys could have been suffering from pretty much anything. West Nile virus had not been active in the region in years, and Lyme disease, though a possibility, was unlikely to have struck such a broad swath of boys. A pair of ambulances slipped into Camp Elk Horn by an overgrown hunting trail, sirens and flashing lights turned off so as not to panic the rest of the campers.

Robbie and I, who as yet showed no symptoms of the terrible sickness, were whisked off to the infirmary for observation and for our own safety. Neither of us had a temperature or swollen glands or loss of appetite or anything of concern in our blood or urine that would suggest we had been infected by whatever the boys were suffering from. When asked by the gray-faced medical examiner if the boys had ingested anything unusual: wild mushrooms, berries, roots, tree bark, we said no. But when pressed by the medical examiner, who wore a shining stethoscope at his chest, if the boys had participated in any out-of-the-ordinary activities during the past few days, Robbie was silent, terrified. His blood had come back revealing high levels of THC within the last twenty-four hours. He had broken camp policy and was in line to be fired and criminally charged for his misdeeds if his results were reported to the camp administration.

"The boys," I said, "found some old bones in the woods."

"Bones?" the medical examiner said, his attention sharp.

"I believe they belonged to a camper who went missing back in the early eighties. His body was never found."

When I woke late the next morning in my tiny infirmary cot, I learned that the camp had been shut down for the rest of the summer, and that those who were not in quarantine had been bused to area hospitals to undergo batteries of tests.

The Great Lawn was empty, the flag flew at half-mast. The cabin windows of the junior campers were dark. The entire camp had disappeared overnight. I ran into Jane, the arts and crafts teacher and a friend of Cathy's, lugging a duffel bag and a tangle of macramé, and asked her what was going on. She broke into violent tears, "Three boys died overnight. They just shriveled up and died."

I held her in my arms and felt her heart pounding against my chest. I wondered which boys had died. It didn't really matter to me—they were all just kids at the beginning of their life journey. After a moment, Jane pulled away and wiped her eyes. "Cathy wants you to Facebook her."

And then Jane was gone, leaving me alone in a ghost town that was just a few days earlier a vibrant, vital summer camp full of laughter and joy.

The boys' cabins had been cordoned off with yellow police tape and the county sheriff's SUV sat parked in a ditch between Owl Bunk and Wolf Bunk. An ambulance idled outside the boys' bunks, its back door swung fully open. Several deputies and assorted county officials milled about talking quietly. I stepped over the tape and made my way toward the cabin. I was afraid of what I would find—I had comforted these boys when they were homesick, when they had wet their beds, when they had failed their swimming tests, when their confused young hearts had been broken for the first time, but I needed my wallet, my phone, the keys to my apartment. I didn't care about the rest of my things, but I wasn't going anywhere with what I had on me at the moment: a laminated staff card and a blue and yellow lanyard bracelet.

An officer in dark aviator glasses and a black Stetson hat stopped me, hands against my chest, as if a verbal order could not possibly be enough to communicate that I could go no further.

"I need to get my things."

"This area is off-limits."

I told him who I was and explained my situation. I couldn't get back to the city without my wallet, and he nodded his head sympathetically and excused himself.

I was left standing out there in the hot sun batting a yellow tetherball back and forth and was reminded of the first day of camp when I had met my ten boys. They were not extraordinary athletes, not prodigies of any kind. They were not yet handsome, stuck somewhere between deep childhood and the guileless splendor of adolescence. They told the same types of silly vulgar jokes that I had told at their age, and they never ever imagined that harm could come to any one of them. It was unthinkable. I had felt the same way when I was a boy until 9/11 struck and then all I thought about for a long time was all the terrible ways one could die.

The deputy returned and said he would get my stuff for me if I could tell him exactly where to find it; he had to be quick. That would be easy. I kept all my personal belongings in a wooden cubby beside my bed. None of my boys ever dared breach my privacy.

As I waited again, the tetherball swinging around and around the aluminum pole like a planet in a rush to circle the sun, I saw the door of Owl Bunk swing open amid urgent shouts and orders. It had been so quiet until that moment that I had allowed my body to relax in the warm sun, to forget the horror behind those wooden walls. A broad-chested EMT with a baby blue cloth mask fastened over his mouth held the door open with his back. A moment later, a stretcher appeared with one of my boys on it. I moved closer to catch a look to see if he was all right, and as the orderlies rushed toward the waiting ambulance, the light blanket they had thrown over his form blew off and fell to the ground.

I wish I had never laid eyes on what I saw then. I didn't even know whose body it was, it was so desiccated, so dried out, so brittle. It looked like a shrunken husk of something completely wasted away. It no longer looked human. The deputy returned, tsk-tsked me, and turned my face away with his gloved hand. "You don't want to see this."

"What happened?"

"That's for the epidemiologist to determine."

"Are they . . . ?" I began.

"You'd better leave," he said, and slipped my things into my hands.

Thirty-one boys died, all of Owl Bunk and all the boys of Wolf Bunk as well as several other boys. Six girls died, and the program director succumbed after three days of struggle. It was believed that everyone who died had come into contact with the bones found out in the woods. But I had held the tiny skull in my hands, and I was alive.

When I returned to the city, I had trouble settling back into my old life; drinking with my school friends seemed a pathetic waste of time, ubiquitous video games a waste of life. I moved alone into a small studio apartment in time for the fall semester and scoured the internet daily for answers. Just after Labor Day the Centers for Disease Control in Atlanta reported they discovered nothing abnormal in their findings. The bones contained nothing out of the ordinary. The kids had died of some sort of fast-moving wasting disease. But its provenance was simply a mystery that had no answer.

The kids' parents blamed the camp and deadly microorganisms and poorly filtered drinking water; they blamed listeria, E. coli and salmonella, but there was no hard evidence to prove anything. They were simply flailing in the dark with the hope of striking something.

I couldn't concentrate on my classes, and I monitored the sympathy pages that had sprung up on Facebook. The kids' parents wrote long messages to their children as if they were still alive. "Hey, champ: I thought of you today when I passed our basketball court." It broke my heart to read them, but I read them and reread them and reread them. I thought about taking my life. What kind of world do we live in where such a thing can happen? Why was I spared?

One day I saw a brief message from Amanda Morrow (née Slater). Mandy. She wrote the type of platitudes one utters when there truly are no words. I clicked on her profile and saw that she lived in Connecticut, outside Hartford, several hours away. I found the lanyard bracelet in my desk drawer, looking as new as the day it was knotted, and suddenly felt the need to meet her and return the bracelet. Perhaps she could help me understand the impossible. I messaged her and explained who I was, and she wrote back within the hour telling me to come anytime.

Thirty years may have passed, and Mandy was married to an insurance executive, a mother of three with twin boys and a girl wearing her down, but she had lost none of her beauty. Her blue eyes were warm and welcoming, her frosted hair cut into a crisp bob. She hugged me in the doorway of her charming white colonial, though I was a complete stranger. She invited me in. It was lunchtime and we sat in silence at her kitchen table, sipping hot tea.

"I'm so sorry," she said at last.

I pulled the lanyard bracelet from my pocket and flattened it out on the table.

"Oh," she said. "I'd forgotten about that."

I told her it had still been fastened to his wrist when we found him, but it slipped off as the boys grabbed his bones up like they were toys. "I thought you should have it," I said. "It only seemed right. You were kind to him."

"I wasn't kind, not kind enough," she said, looking away, her eyes misting. "Before that awful night when he disappeared, I called him those names, too, not to his face, but in my mind. He was so skinny; it was frightening to look at him. So, he was Biafran Man. I didn't even know what that meant at the time, but I knew it wasn't kind." She was silent, sipping her green tea. "When I returned home, I went to the public library to learn what Biafran Man could possibly mean, and oh, I felt sick to my stomach. I felt so guilty."

I had looked up Biafra on Wikipedia before my first summer at Camp Elk Horn, having heard about the local legend who had disappeared into nothingness, and I had read about the Nigerian Civil War in which hundreds of thousands of children from the breakaway Republic of Biafra, maybe more than one million, had been systematically starved to death. It had been all over the news in the early '70s and someone at Camp Elk Horn remembered the horror and widened the circle of pain through their cruel words. I found a picture of a tiny baldheaded boy with giant wet eyes and a huge head heavy on his thin neck, his arms barely twigs, his belly distended with hunger. *Biafran Man*—surely the cruelest nickname I had ever heard.

"He knew what it meant," Mandy said. "He was a smart kid. He knew. He was such a great dancer, so free. He came alive for the first time all summer when we danced. Afterward, we walked back to my cabin. I wanted to give him something—the bracelet, so he would always know he had a friend. His wrist was so thin it kept slipping off, so I had to re-knot it twice. He had been afraid those boys would really hurt him, but he said he wasn't afraid, not anymore, with me as his friend. He swore to me as he left my cabin that night that he would make them all sorry for how they treated him. They would all pay. They were brave words, but I knew they were empty threats uttered simply to make himself feel better. But now, I believe he really did have his revenge."

"But these weren't the same kids," I said.

She was quiet for a moment, "Do you really think they would have acted any different?"

I was stunned for a moment when I realized I had no idea. My kids weren't cruel kids; they weren't sadistic, mean-spirited people; they'd been known on occasion to get ahead of logic and reason, their rampant insecurities taking over, but they would have treated a stranger in their midst better. I had to believe that, or simply give up on the whole human enterprise.

"What about me?" I said. "Would I have acted any different when I was a boy?"

"You?" she said taking my wrist and slipping the lanyard bracelet on, tying a tight knot at my pulse. "You would have done the right thing. Don't you think?"

THE CINQ À SEPT GIRL

It had been nearly a year since Chloe graduated and moved to Boston to work as an artist's assistant for a painter she had admired since she was a girl. She'd first seen his canvases up close on a school trip to the Musée des Beaux-Arts and had been overcome with breathless admiration and awe, her mouth flooding with bitter saliva.

She imagined she would learn at the knee of the master who would praise her work, impart precious wisdom earned over a lifetime in the trenches of the art world. Chloe had thought their interactions would be alternately flirtatious, sexual, and teacherly. But he was moody, pretentious, and temperamental. They rarely spoke, and she never actually saw him paint. His clothing stank of stale cigarettes. When he needed his brushes cleaned or a canvas stretched or any number of empty tasks, he texted her curt instructions from the other side of his studio. Chloe was certain he intended to chew her up and vomit her back out without ever teaching her a thing. She wondered if he even knew her name. He refused to give her a key, and was often late, leaving her standing in the rain waiting for him to arrive to let her in.

Boston was a dead carcass of a city still haunted by its Puritan past. Back home in Montréal, Chloe would just be going out as the bars and clubs in Boston were closing for the night. She was shocked how Bostonians dressed without any attempt at style or whimsy or sensuality, how their joyless, pinched faces ignored each other on the street. She had no real friends. The world to her began to feel like an unanswered telephone—lonesome, empty, and full of unquenchable longing.

When she met David in the cocktail lounge of a hotel off Copley Square, a quiet, wood-paneled bar that never had more than ten people in it, she knew right away, despite his platinum wedding band and silver hair, she would do anything he asked. "We desire prohibited things precisely because they are prohibited," Chloe thought. She felt the tightness of want in her mouth, like biting into a sour fruit.

He was older than her father, marathon-fit, a year or two either side of sixty, six feet tall with a full head of hair and all his own teeth. In the jeweled light thrown from Tiffany-style lamps hanging above the bar, he was devastatingly handsome. But she didn't care what he looked like. Ugly and beautiful were the same thing to Chloe.

In the hotel room, overlooking the Charles River and the flickering lights of Cambridge, he bit her neck and shoulders, pulled her long brown hair until her scalp burned, and pushed her face into the pillow. She was grateful that he didn't ask her what she wanted. He was not wracked by the usual self-conscious insecurities of men her own age who had grown up watching porn on the internet. He knew how to take his time.

"I want you to do anything you want to me," she said. "I want you to be mean to me. I want you to hurt me."

She had skin the color of the original generation of wandering desert sinners who never made it to the Promised Land, but when she returned to her apartment that first night, her thighs and hips and ass and neck were purple with fresh bruises.

David said he was a managing partner at one of Boston's oldest blue-blood law firms and lived in a gated estate somewhere west of the city. After meeting twice a week for several months in what soon came to be *their suite,* that was all she knew of him. At first, she was pleased she didn't have to suffer the requisite tales of childhood traumas, heartaches, failures, clichéd troubles at home or work. She was exhausted by most men's misguided idea of intimacy. No woman true to her desires wants to mother her lover.

She filled her empty evenings with David.

He tied her down to the bed and gagged her with her dirty underwear and fucked her for a long time, finishing on her face. He slapped her ass, pulled her hair like a horse's bridle, choked her.

"Harder," she managed to gasp. "Squeeze harder."

With his large hands firm at her throat, manicured thumb and forefinger forming a viselike V at her larynx, she was nothing, and she was everything, both at the same time. The gurgled sounds she made were barely human—part beast, part angel. She knew she could disappear forever from this bullshit life if he pressed just a little harder, a little longer.

One night as they lay stretched out across the king-sized bed, he said, with proper Brahmin locution, that he had an offer for her, and she could take as long as she needed to answer.

"I own an apartment in Beacon Hill. An old pied-à-terre I haven't used in years. The last tenants moved months ago. I want you to live there. I will come see you after work every Tuesday and Thursday, with the exception of Thanksgiving and Christmas week and the second half of August. The rest of the time, you can do whatever you wish with whomever you want. You owe me nothing else."

Chloe kissed him on the face and lips and said, "Yes."

He returned her kiss with a parched tongue and said, "I will not see you any other time. And I owe you nothing. Is that perfectly clear?"

Chloe had grown up in the lush, moneyed enclave of Westmount, but had spent her entire adult life living in crappy, crooked-floored flats with roommates and cats and beer bottles and pizza boxes stacked in the kitchen, both in Notre-Dame-de-Grâce and the student ghetto of Allston. So, when she moved into his elegant apartment on Beacon Hill with its dove-gray walls and gleaming wooden floors, she felt she was finally starting to live the life she deserved.

Chloe rarely desired to leave except to perform her labors for the artist; she ordered in Thai or Indian nearly every night and fell asleep alone with a thick novel dog-eared on her chest, sometimes Dostoyevsky, sometimes David Foster Wallace, and sometimes, her guilty pleasure, Stephen King. Most nights she luxuriated in her deep claw-footed bathtub, drinking whatever single malt he had left behind the last time, wondering what he was doing at that very moment. Sometimes, a few drinks in, she wanted to call him just to hear his calm, measured voice. But she had no phone number for him, not his cell phone which he locked with a carefully guarded password, not his office, and not his home. She had once rifled his wallet when he was showering her scent from his body, and found only a thick bundle of crisp bills, arranged by denomination, all facing the same way, and an unstamped rewards card from a local coffee shop, any evidence of identification removed.

Now that she had her own address, he never showed up empty-handed. He brought her a pair of Christian Louboutin kid leather six-inch black pumps and ordered her to strip and put them on right away. The shoes were designed to force the insole over the heel, so she had to walk on the balls of her feet, tilting forward, with her calf muscles tensed to keep balanced. She had learned to walk in heels even before her bat mitzvah and had little difficulty strutting across the floor to kneel before him and take his dick in her mouth. When he was done, he told her to never wear those shoes outside the bedroom. That was fine by her; she couldn't bear the thought of scuffing the arterial red of the soles.

He brought her beautiful things—stockings trimmed in lace and so sheer that she couldn't stand up in them without tearing them, perfume that smelled tart, like a grapefruit. Dark red lipstick in a gold case shaped like a bullet. He brought her a vintage brocaded black corset which left her small breasts exposed when fastened. He cinched the boning tight at the waist, so it hurt Chloe to take a breath, and when he fucked her from behind, he pulled on the laces, and she cried out in pain. She knew she could only love a man who could hurt her, because only he could take away her pain.

The hours away from him pressed on her, and she felt distracted and headachy. She would buy a ticket for a movie at the Brattle Theatre and leave halfway through, unable to remember what she'd just seen. She had trouble finishing books, and started sketch after sketch, only to abandon it.

She wondered what the world looked like through David's frigid blue eyes. What did he fear when he lay his head down to sleep at night? She wondered about the school ring he never took off, or whether he ever noticed that the freckled pattern of tiny moles on his chest vaguely resembled the shape of Ursa Minor. When she asked him what he was thinking, he did not respond, left her words untouched in the darkness between them.

When he arrived at her apartment the following Tuesday, a bottle of Camus Cuvée cognac tucked under his arm, and she asked how his day was, he said it was fine, thank you, and when she followed with a cheery, "Tell me everything that has happened since I last saw you," David said she was beautiful.

He may as well have tossed acid in her face.

"I want you to be real for me," she said. "I am real."

"Not once I leave this room."

"Look at me. Touch me. I matter!"

He nodded politely and slipped the strap from her dress. "Shall we get started?"

"Wait," she said, drowning. "I'm trying to talk to you."

"Need I remind you, that is not what we agreed to."

She had known the sublime pain of heartbreak many times before, but never, never had she felt this, something she could only describe as soulbreak. It is hard to cry when someone is watching you. She sniffled and smeared the back of her hand against her nose.

"Are you done?"

"Yes."

"Go wash your face."

The artist had hired a new assistant right out of RISD, a tattooed poseur named Bree with bleached dreadlocks and Clark Kent glasses. During Chloe's tenure, the artist had treated all his other apprentices with equal contempt, and they had tearfully cycled through his studio with predictable haste. But Bree was different. She and the artist laughed conspiratorially, shared workspace and ordered in brown rice sushi every day for lunch. Chloe had always assumed he was gay, but now she was convinced the artist was sleeping with Bree.

Chloe approached the artist. "Damien, I'd like to speak with you."

Was that an eye roll Chloe saw, a knowing wink between him and Bree? "What is it?""In private."

"This is as private as it gets, sweetheart. You've already entered the Holy of Holies."

Bree stood nearby, her pale cheeks dimpling in anticipation of a throwdown.

"I've been here a long time and I've done everything you've asked without complaint. I show up on time and I never leave early. But sometimes it feels like I'm working on an assembly line. I can do this with my eyes closed."

"Is that all?"

"No, that's not all," Chloe said. "I want to do more than mix your colors and glaze your paintings and prepare your work to hang for exhibition. I want you to talk to me, share your knowledge with me. I'm a painter, too, you know. I'm better than this."

"Perhaps things would be different if you worked with your eyes open."

Bree let out an ugly, convulsive laugh.

"What are you talking about?"

"You stroll in here every day like you're Miss Thang, like the world owes you a living because you say you are an artist. But you have nothing to offer me, and I have nothing to offer you. I give you a gold star sticker for hanging on this long, but that's all I have to give. Most princesses like you would have quit a long time ago."

Chloe went to Savenor's Market on Charles Street and bought a fresh Colorado lamb crown roast. At DeLuca's market she bought fresh rosemary and pearl potatoes and organic spring vegetables. She chose a selection of artisan cheeses and a clutch of grapes to accompany an expensive bottle of bordeaux.

She spent the day in the kitchen preparing dinner for David, sure that she was done in plenty of time to shower, slip naked into a clean apron and a pair of heels and greet him at the door. She imagined them sitting around the laden dinner table sipping wine, laughing drily about what an asshole the artist was and how she'd be better off without him. "Onward and upward," he would say, or something like that. She envisioned the two of them fucking right on top of their dirty plates, silverware, denuded lamb bones, glasses crashing to the floor all around them.

Chloe adjusted the dishes on the table, changing the angle of the wine bottle until the light from the lamp shone through it. Crystal from the cabinet that she'd never used, white cloth napkins.

David arrived at precisely five o'clock as always. The table was laid, the wine breathing appropriately. "How was your day?" Chloe said, rising on her toes to kiss him on the cheek in mock imitation of a good wife.

She at least expected him to laugh or smile or say something complimentary about the first meal she had ever made for him, but he only said, "You know I haven't time for this."

"But I spent all day preparing this meal."

He held out a flat, lavender-colored cardboard box, *La Perla* written across the lid in looping silver script. "Put this on."

In the bed, she crouched on her hands and knees, the negligee pushed up to her waist. She felt clammy and cold and ugly, squatting like a frog as he pushed himself into her. The smell of the lamb roast burning in the oven sickened Chloe. She had saved her appetite all day to fully savor the meal with David. When he grabbed for her hair when he began to come, she lifted her mouth to his shoulder and sank her teeth into his skin as hard as she possibly could. In that moment, she was prepared to be a cannibal, to chew and gnaw at him and eat him alive. He snarled and hit the back of her head, but his flesh was springy between her teeth, and she felt a bone-deep ache in her jaw and clamped down harder. She would not let go even as he hammered her in the face with his fists, even as he shrieked in pain. The coppery taste of his hot blood made her bite down harder, clamping her jaws shut on him until he squeezed her windpipe, and she fell back onto the pillow. David had warned Chloe time and again about scratching and biting and pinching—he could do as he pleased with her, but she was to leave no mark on him anywhere. There was no way he could hide this wound from his wife, and Chloe smiled as he regarded the deep punctures in his spa-perfect skin.

"You're a sick, deeply disturbed woman. You know that?"

"I was hungry," she said, fresh blood and bits of gore dripping from her lips.

Chloe knew he'd come back, and even when he didn't show the following Tuesday, she knew David would return for more.

She found a small expensive stationery shop on Newbury Street, where she bought a set of pearl-gray note paper, hand-pressed, lightly frayed edges, thick envelopes. He would appreciate these. No doubt his wife wrote her thank-you notes on paper just like this, with elegant private school-girl handwriting. She watched the salesgirl carefully wrap her purchase in tissue as though it were jewelry, and impulsively bought a sleek silver pen with a gold nib to go with it.

At home, she wrote three copies of the same note explaining exactly how she had died and by whose hand, restarting every time she made an error or held the pen still for too long, making the ink bleed through the paper. She tucked each of the delicate pages into its own envelope. Then she also slipped a copy of the sketches she had made of him into each envelope and licked them. Even the glue tasted expensive. She carried them downstairs to the mailbox and watched them drop down the slot.

David arrived exactly at five. She greeted him with a smile and kissed him softly on the lips. "Mea maxima culpa," she said. "How's your arm?"

"Healing."

When they had stripped for what would be the last time, Chloe saw beneath the cotton bandage, the extent of the damage she had done to his shoulder. It was a monstrous wound that looked like it had been stitched by a butcher. The ugly sutures reminded her of a flattened spider or desiccated caterpillar laid out on a hot summer sidewalk. She wanted to unstring the stitches and finger fuck the deep cavity of his wound, until he came a spray of brilliant blood all over her face. But he was fucking her now, all his pent-up aggression concentrated in his hard-thrusting hips.

"Put your hands on my neck," she whispered.

He did exactly as she asked.

"Harder," she said. "I want you to hurt me like I hurt you."

And when he complied, she gasped, "Harder." She felt her throat constrict, her tongue going stiff against her teeth, as she breathed her last air of this rotten world, neurons firing a twenty-one gun salute, adrenaline flooding every cell of her body with the glorious nullifier dopamine, and then something cracked, a tiny bone in her neck perhaps, or was it the very seams of the world tearing open, washing her with everlasting joy, a bright, throbbing tunnel of darkness opening before her like the doorway to eternal life.

FUCK ALMIGHTY

I didn't know fuck-all about nothin' the summer I worked as a Shabbos goy at Cantor's Regency Hotel and Spa, a tarnished never-was-nothin' jewel right in the buckle of the Borscht Belt. It may have been a hundred-mile razor cut from Flatbush and the Loews King's Theater where I tore fifty-cent tickets Friday nights, but with the green trees and fresh mountain air, I coulda been in Timbuktu for all I knew.

I was sixteen years old and built like a concrete shit-house with a choice Dion and the Belmonts' pompadour, scarred up knuckles, and a college school ring I'd lifted from the theater's coat check. I wore it on my wedding ring finger as a sort of fuck you to the whole life-sentence institution. If my folks' never-ending title fight of a marriage was any clue of the future waiting for me, I'd take the electric chair any day of the week.

The night before I left, Dicky handed me a Trojan and said, "Joosh broads is easy. Nonnadat Catlicker guilt on dem Talmudical brains."

I'd copped a feel here and there but was still cherry as the first day on earth, not an inch of snatch to speak of and it looked like the summer was going to go off that way. The big shot husbands ordered me around like a dog:

"do this, boy," "do that," "faster! faster!" "Those are Dunlop tennis rackets, not kindling," "Are you deaf or just stupid?" In my burgundy blazer with gold piping on the sleeves, I looked like a captain who'd lost his ship. I hated what I was becoming: a worn out stiff like my miserable old man.

I learned to make myself scarce when the men was around and kissed up to the wives, smiling a million-dollar smile every time I schlepped their luggage. Sometimes when they slipped a folded dollar bill into my hand, they gave a squeeze and batted their masqueraded lashes, flashing their yellow teeth like they would devour me whole.

Halfway through the summer, with no prime tail to chase, I was staring down another endless stretch of lonesome knuckle fucking. I'd pounded my prick so raw it ached every time it shifted in my jockeys.

Fuckface Ira Silverman, the head bellhop, was busy chatting up some skirt like he was Doctor Kildare and told me to take up a couple brandy Stingers up to 212 and to make it snappy. I was too young to serve booze but couldn't stand the sight of that hatchet-faced feeb sweet talking the only true prospect I'd seen all week.

The dim hallway stank of stale cigarettes and a kind of permanent punch-in-the-nose mildew. Freddy Cannon's "Palisades Park" played on the transistor radio behind the door and right away I knew something was different, because the old Jews always seemed to be screaming at each other even when they wasn't. I blew into my palm to check my breath, because you never knew what prize might be waiting behind door number one.

I knocked and a soft voice told me it's open.

I could have shit myself right there, because in each of the two twin beds a beehived, bottle blonde knockout is laying beneath the covers with her perfect naked titties sitting there like snow cones on display at Luna Park. The girl to my right is out cold so I says to the other, bending low with my tray out, "I got your cocktails."

I can't take my eyes off her tits and my nuts are about to bust.

"Whatsyername?" she says.

"Frank."

"Frank's a nice name. I got a uncle Frank upstate somewheres."

I'm holding the tray out and trying not to stare at her cans but they're like magnets pulling my eyes like I'm some hungry cartoon wolf.

"You like them?" she says.

"Yeah," I tell her. "They're real pretty."

She looks at me with blank blue eyes and says, "You got a girl back home?"

"Stag as the day is long," I say.

"Good," she says.

The rubber in my pocket is tickling my nuts. I'm so hard you could've hung a lantern on my prick that would've lit the whole world. I skip right past missionary and picture me and her doing it doggie style and she's moaning my name like it's a secret she just discovered.

She takes the Stinger off the tray, offering the other drink with a twist of her delicate wrist.

"It's finally happening," I think. "This is it!"

She clicks my glass with hers and says, "May the good Lord take a liking to you . . . but not too soon!"

She downs her drink in one swallow. I do the same and it burns like Sunday morning hellfire.

"You're not Jewish?" I say.

"Ever see a Jewish nun?"

I look at her but her words don't make no sense. But my hard-on knows enough to curl up and die. Her tits may as well be behind glass in a museum for all the good they'll do me.

She says, "Me an' Misty is joining the Sisters of the Immaculate Virgin."

She's maybe twenty-one and don't look nothing like Sister Angela with her pushed-in face and beard hairs, and I ask her why she'd do a thing like that.

Del Shannon's "Runaway" is playing, and it is the saddest song I ever heard. Their two pink Samsonites sit packed by the door, and I want to tell her not to do it, the church will take her entire life and won't give nothin' back. I just want her to stay with me and never leave.

"Why?" I say.

"I'm tired," she says.

"Let me go with you," I say.

She laughs, kinda sad like.

And then I say, "You got an address for the convent? Maybe I can write you a letter or something."

She smiles a hurting smile and says, "You're real cute, Frank. If I'd'a met you a year ago we'd of had a lot of fun."

GALLERY OF THE DISAPPEARED MEN

She had seen that clouded look before, a determined mix of pity and revulsion and something else she could not define. It was there and then gone in an instant, like that first surprising zing of life she had felt in her belly all those months back. She had seen that expression nine times in her thirty-one years, and every time, it meant one thing: that he was leaving. Now, with that little grim-faced gangster squalling in the bed next to her, crying for the milk that seeped from her swollen breasts, she knew that she had never deserved it more.

Josh had promised he would stand beside her, and never go below the waist. There would be tearing and stretching and blood, and she was afraid he would never want to touch her again. He had kept his word during twelve hours of labor, holding her hand as she cursed and wept with the rolling of the contractions. He fed her ice chips and mopped sweat from her brow when she vomited into the plastic bedpan. But when it came time to push, he had grabbed the camera from his overnight bag and stationed himself beside the doctor at the foot of the birthing table.

The baby was fever-bright and ugly, and reminded her of a shrunken squint-eyed *zayde* or a tomato-can boxer who'd taken one too many lumps in the ring. Through the uprights of her numbed legs, she could see Josh reaching out for the thing, scissors in hand to cut the cord. And then she saw it, as the sustaining jellyfish of her placenta slid onto the table, behind the sympathetic glow of his smile, something ever so subtle changed in his face, the shift just long enough for her to register.

The baby had fallen back to sleep as suddenly as it had woken, and through the hum of the baby monitor, she could hear the static-crossed conversations of neighbors on their cordless phones, whispered ghosts reaching out from an undertow of darkness. In the empty place in her belly, she felt the undeniable truth that while she had been sleeping, her husband had left her.

She called to him but was answered only by the swish of broken souls crackling through the monitor on her dresser. "Josh!" she called, louder this time, her rising voice tossing the baby in his fragile sleep. She climbed out of bed, pulled her robe tight around herself and went downstairs.

The living room was empty. Through the bay window, she could see bright snow falling in the street. She stood for a long time, desolate, her face pressed to the cold glass as the snow fell before her. She felt a familiar sense of anger, shame, and loneliness, but she would not let herself cry. Not again.

The TV was on in the basement, tuned to a hockey game. She unlatched the baby gate and crept down the carpeted stairs. Someone was sitting on the couch. He looked familiar to her but had changed over the years. She considered the mathematical possibilities that Daniel would show up in her basement after all this time, and her jagged formula only increased her certitude that it was him.

"Amy. What are you doing out of bed? Where is the baby?"

One time, she and Daniel had kissed in the falling snow, a fat flake melting on his long eyelashes as he told her that he'd found a real girlfriend who was prettier and would do more than just French kiss him.

"Did you leave the baby alone on the bed?"

He had sat behind her in history class and kicked at her chair whenever Mr. Gillick faced the blackboard. He looked so old now, his face creased with concern, his hair graying at his temples. What sweet revenge that he had aged while she had stayed the same.

"There's no baby, dumbass. All we ever did was make out a couple of times in your parents' basement."

"Amy, what is the matter?"

"You're ugly, Daniel" she said. "I always thought you were ugly. But now, you look like an old man. I was never going to do it with you, you know."

Daniel stepped forward to embrace her and she pushed him away with a force that was surprising even to her.

"Don't you touch me, or I'll tell Missy that you're two-timing her."

Now, he spoke very slowly and deliberately, as if he really were afraid Amy was going to rat him out to his new girlfriend.

"Amy. Listen. You're exhausted. You need your sleep." He led her to the couch, unfolded a colorful afghan and draped it over her. "I'm going upstairs to check on the baby. You stay here. I'll be right back."

She sat shivering with an inexplicable heat and squeezed her eyes together to force Daniel from her mind. When she opened her eyes later, she was reassured by the sight of her father's familiar oversized hiking boots standing sentry by the back door. She heard footsteps through the baby monitor and climbed the stairs.

Her father stood in the center of the bedroom, rocking the baby in his arms. He had not shaved and the placid look on his face mocked her.

"The baby's dead," she said flatly.

His head jolted up. "Amy," he said. "Why would you say such an awful thing?"

"He's dead. The baby's dead. He went to sleep and didn't wake up. I remember. I remember everything."

"Honey, you're confused. This is Jack, our baby, not your brother."

"No, no, no!" she screamed. "Don't lie to me. You got drunk and left him on his stomach. He turned blue and died in his sleep and now you're going away forever."

As if solely for the purpose of humiliating her, he unwrapped the wailing pink thing and held it out to her. Its thin little legs were folded up into its body like a frog waiting to spring.

"You switched him with someone else. That's not mine. That creature is not mine. Not mine," she sobbed.

He stroked her hair and wiped away a tear with his thumb. "Shhh," he whispered in her ear. "It's going to be all right."

"Get that thing away from me," she said, pulling away from him.

"He's our son. You wanted him so badly."

"Get rid of him. Flush him down the toilet. Just get him out of my sight."

He left the room and appeared shortly thereafter. "I've swaddled him and he's resting in his crib with his binky. Now are you going to tell me what the hell is going on?"

"You smell like vomit," she said.

"Amy, please, just tell me what's the matter."

"Don't patronize me, David. All right?"

"David? I'm not David."

"Then who are you?"

She felt fear tightening in the back of her neck at the possibility that she had no idea who this man was. She felt ridiculous and suddenly very delicate. Her heart beat fiercely in her chest. But it was David. She was certain because of the arrogant way he cocked his right eyebrow when he thought he was right.

"I'm calling Dr. Sharma. You need help. I know this isn't you, Amy. We read about this. It's just an explosion of hormones racing through your body and messing with your neurotransmitters."

"Don't talk to me about hormones, you misogynist pig. I'm pregnant, David. I'm pregnant."

"I'm calling Dr. Sharma right now."

"That's right, go call your back-alley doctor. I'd hate to ruin your fancy law school plans. Don't look at me like that. I know what that look means."

Amy rushed to the bathroom and closed the door, her thoughts overrunning each other in searing waves. She knew he was going to burst in any minute, so she scrambled through the medicine cabinet until she found the crumpled cardboard box with the last remaining test. She peed on the stick. If she could prove to David that she was carrying his child, he could never leave. The devastating result appeared moments later in the form of an X in the tiny window. She curled up on the floor beside the toilet and, through the heating vent, overheard him talking on the telephone about emotional stress and strange, frightening behavior. She knew what she had to do.

The baby lay bundled in a green blanket beneath a simple black-and-white mobile that provided the effect of M.C. Escher's flying birds gradually transforming themselves into swimming fish. He was hot like a coal from the fireplace, and she tucked him under her arm and inched toward the top of the stairs.

Amy heard something about antipsychotic medications, whisper-shouts into the mouthpiece of the telephone, as she slipped past the kitchen and unlocked the front door. The snow continued to fall from the sky in sticky, thick clumps and she stepped out onto the icy pavement in her bare feet. There was one thing she had to do and that was run as fast as she could.

By the time she reached the end of the street, she'd counted six houses that still had their Christmas lights burning. A half-inflated Santa Claus bobbed lethargically in the wind. If only she could find her house, her mother would be waiting with hot cocoa and a cozy blanket; she knew it was around here somewhere, but in the storm, she could no longer tell which way she was running. The bundle she clutched in her arms was howling, and something told her that if she could just dump it in a snowbank, she could fly through the frozen streets unburdened, right into the warmth of her mother's kitchen.

She found a sharp drift of snow and began digging out a hollow with her free hand. The bundle shrieked and squirmed in her other arm.

A car pulled up behind her, honking its horn. She shivered, her clenched fists raw. She wanted to run, but her legs were stiff with cold.

"Amy," a voice called from the open car window. "Amy. What are you doing out here? Where's the baby!"

The wind had risen; it seemed to be getting more frigid by the instant. As she stood in the blowing snow, she wondered how she had arrived here. She felt a terrible anguish grip her chest. What had she done?

She heard a baby sobbing, crimson-faced, and felt the warmth of an overcoat enrobing her and the insistent heat of dry lips at her face. "It's me. Josh. Your husband."

"You're Josh."

"Yes, yes. Josh. Remember the time we got lost in the snow in Bishops Forest, and I gave you my coat and we found our way out."

She felt calmed inside his coat, two hearts beating against her chest, one tiny and fragile and one almost too big and brave for this world. "You got pneumonia."

"Yes," Josh said. "I did."

"For me." She smiled.

"Yes," he said.

"Josh," she pleaded. "Don't leave me. Please tell me you won't ever, ever leave me."

"I won't, Amy. I won't ever, ever leave you. That's a promise."

ADAM NUMBER THREE

Adam Number Three found the hand in Forest Grove ravine under a pile of dry leaves by the slow-moving stream where he liked to skip rocks. It was a grown-up's hand, with dark, stiff hair on the knuckles and a gold ring on the swollen finger next to the pinky. Its nails were dirty and cracked and broken and Adam poked the hand with a pointed stick. The hand was pale and freckled, its thick, sausage fingers upturned as if expecting change from a clerk at the 7-Eleven. He flicked the hand around with his stick and saw where it had been cut off neatly at the wrist. The bloody bone and marrow and veins and all the other gross stuff would have freaked out most kids in his class, but he didn't mind. Adam knew it was just a hand removed from its body, and it couldn't hurt him.

Adam emptied out his lunch box, slurped down two yogurt tubes, and tossed the wrappers into the stream. He laid his lunch box down on the ground and maneuvered the hand inside with the toe of his shoe. The icepack was still cold from that morning.

He determined he would find out who the hand belonged to but thought better of it when he realized that canvassing his neighborhood would mean leaving behind the safety of the forest. The other kids would ruin everything.

He was the third Adam in his class, and last in the alphabet behind Adam Carlson and Adam Elliot, so Ms. Drake and his classmates simply called him Adam Number Three, or sometimes just Number Three. James O'Hara, who gave him an atomic wedgie once after gym class, just called him "Three."

Adam planned to spend his entire summer down in the cool shade of the ravine, reading books and imagining a life without those nasty boys. It wasn't his fault he had red hair and a big nose. It wasn't his fault he had asthma and carried that goofy inhaler everywhere he went. And it wasn't his fault his dad ran off forever, leaving him alone with his mom when he was three years old.

Adam could not understand what the other kids thought was so funny about all that. His mother told him he had his grandfather's nose, and that red hair made him special. He liked to laugh as well, but never seemed to laugh at the same things as the rest of his class.

Sometimes it got lonely in the ravine, and he wished he had somebody to talk to. He opened the lunchbox and regarded the hand. The fine lines on the palm told a story: the heart line, the head line, and the life line, but he had no idea how to read those lines. It looked like a friendly hand, and he imagined who it had belonged to.

Before he and his mother moved away, there was a nice man named Mr. Smart who lived next door and taught Adam about annuals and perennials and soil and bulbs, how to identify weeds, and how to tell the difference between harmful grubs and friendly worms. They tilled the soil together and planted beans and tomatoes and lettuce in Mr. Smart's garden. He told Adam he had a green thumb just like his son had when he was a little boy. One night, Adam's mother woke him from a deep sleep and said they had to leave now. He never saw the tomatoes or beans or lettuce in bloom, and he never saw Mr. Smart again. He could see clearly that the hand did not have a green thumb, but he wondered whether it had been as kind a hand as that of Mr. Smart.

Adam knew the original Adam from the Bible had made Eve out of his own rib, so why could he not make a man out of a hand? He dug with his stick in the hard earth beneath the leafy green maple, his arms aching with the effort. Then he found a large sharp-edged rock and hacked away at the earth until he had dug a hole that seemed deep enough.

The bare hole appeared lonely and sad, so he found some wildflowers and tossed them in as a colorful carpet for the hand to lie upon. The bright purples and whites and yellows looked festive, and Adam smiled as he lowered the hand into the hole. He understood that the hand had no mind, no body, but he knew somehow that it appreciated his efforts, and that he would be rewarded for them.

He returned every day to water the hand, to chase off flies and rooting squirrels and assure there was enough sun for it to grow. He filled his Thermos three times with the cool water of the stream and slowly, delicately let it soak the earth. Adam sat by the tree listening to the songbirds and reading Jules Verne and Robert Louis Stevenson and Mark Twain, and he was happy.

Sometimes he heard voices above the ravine, the other boys playing army with their rat-tatting toy guns, their shouts and curses breaking the serenity of his solitude. He spoke to the hand, laying his ear against the earth, his mouth moving slowly as he took his time recounting the happiest moments in his life, his greatest desires, and dreams, hoping soon he would have a friend to keep him company.

One day, during a vicious heat wave, Adam heard the high-pitched voices of the boys coming closer.

"Aw, your mother's a hooker."

"And your dad's a fucktard."

Adam could see them on the narrow footpath now, pulling thin branches off green trees. James O'Hara was in the lead, dark sunglasses covering his eyes. He was followed by Jimmy Regis, Dallas Gray, and another kid whose name was either Douche or Bruce.

Adam thought of hiding, but it didn't feel right to leave the hand alone. This was his ravine after all—the boys had the whole entire rest of the world, so why come down here and spoil everything?

"Hey, assbag, you just stepped on my heel."

"Well, why are you wearing heels? You a girl, huh? A faggot or something?"

They were close enough now that Adam could hear the familiar hollow thud of a fist against a bony chest.

"Ow! You didn't have to do that."

"Did too."

"Did not."

Now, James O'Hara, lifting his sunglasses in joyous disbelief, saw Adam sitting at the foot of the tree.

"Look who's here," he said, turning to his companions. "Three. The loneliest number."

Adam knew it was best to keep silent.

"What are you doing down here? Whacking off?"

The other boys laughed.

"Gimme some water. I'm thirsty as hell," James O'Hara said.

Adam had been planning to water the hand and had already consecrated the water with a private wish that the hand would grow nicely into a fully formed body.

"Get your own," Adam said, surprising himself.

"Did you hear that?" James O'Hara said. "Get my own?"

In an instant he was on top of Adam, pummeling him with his fists, hitting his face and chest and arms. The other boys stood by laughing, kicking dirt in Adam's eyes so he couldn't tell who was hitting him now. Adam always knew that James O'Hara was a dangerous boy like his older brother Jack, with a long life of prison ahead of him, but he could not believe that James was going to kill him right now over something as silly as a sip of water. Before he lost consciousness, Adam wished that if he died, the hand would live and grow and bloom, the offspring of his own loving care.

When Adam came to, the ravine was quiet, still, like the first day on earth; even the birds in the trees seemed to have taken their leave. He felt dizzy and his vision was blurred from the blows to the head, but as he tried to scramble to his feet, he realized he was not alone. A large, hairy-knuckled hand reached out to help him up. It wore the same gold ring as the hand he had buried beneath the tree. Backlit by the sun, Adam could see the man was large, with a thick torso and broad shoulders. He took the man's hand and allowed him to pull him to his feet. He was covered with dirt, and tiny wildflowers had twined themselves through his clothing.

The man did not say a word as Adam gained his balance and saw the awful carnage before him. James O'Hara lay nearby on the ground, his head split nearly in half by the sharp rock Adam had used to dig the hole beneath the maple tree. Dallas Gray hung crookedly from a tree branch, a leather belt fastened around his broken neck. The other two boys were so badly beaten it was impossible to tell which boy was which.

"Oh no! Oh no!" cried Adam. "What happened?"

The man stepped closer, and Adam could see his brutal face for the first time, the deep cruelty of his eyes. "I wanted to thank you—for giving me life."

"No," Adam said. "No. Don't thank me like this. Don't."

"When the judge said I'd get life, I thought he meant something else." The man chuckled, then cleared some dirt out of his ears with a battered finger.

"But why did you kill them?"

"Some people sing, some people dance, some people race cars," the man said. "Killing is the only thing I'm good at."

"That's wrong," Adam said. "That is so wrong. I'm going to have to call the police on you."

The man smiled a misshapen smile that showed his yellow teeth, turned his massive back on Adam, and walked away into the woods.

IN FLAGRANTE DELICTO

She would tell herself years later it was the discovery of the long-forgotten Slut List that changed everything. The simple act of unfolding those crinkled composition book pages had kicked down a locked door into a life in which she had been unbound, free, and bursting with the power of her presumed birthright. The Slut List, in her trembling hands, still faintly scented with dewberry oil and the blind hope of youth, had awakened in Jennifer Walters the dormant, vestigial desire to fuck simply for the sake of fucking.

It had been so long since she had done so without purpose. Nearly six years of marriage to Chris, much of the early years a pathetic burlesque in which she could not get pregnant no matter how she tilted her pelvis, no matter how long she allowed Chris's lazy sperm to marinate in the blazing darkness of her vagina. Later, she rode him gently, slowly, marking slow time against the ticking clock of Chris's malignant brain tumor, giving herself to him to help take his worried mind off the unavoidable truth of his condition.

He was dying, but on his own schedule.

The past week alone Chris had four grand mal seizures, the last of which occurred as Jennifer wept silently, stiffly, beside him, his muscles contracting violently against the bed's stainless steel safety rails.

She had been Jenny Ryan then, and it was Victoria Barber's idea to create a Slut List so that she and Jenny and Cody Griffin with her crimped hair and red painted lips could keep track of their conquests. Studying the list now, and her looping girlish script, she was reminded how easy it had been. No boy had ever said no, and sometimes one of them would foolishly say he loved her, his raw adenoidal voice breaking under the weight of his sincerity.

Jenny had made meticulous notes beside the names of Johnnyboy Rogers, Maris Lukovs, Tim Anderson, Jesse Sanchez and on and on down the list to the short bus kid with the tiny dick from Saint Gabriel's whose name she never learned. She had come up with the symbol ȸ to indicate circumcised penises and the symbol ȹ to designate boys who were uncircumcised, a sort of dicks up/dicks down system like Siskel and Ebert at the movies. It all came back to her with savage clarity: whose come tasted sweet and whose was bitter like bleach, who came too fast, who bit, who slapped her ass, who found her clit, and who was totally clued out. Steve whatshisface wanted to fuck her in the ass, and Michael Javits, the virgin, had cried in her arms when he was done his business.

Chris snored quietly in bed, his pain meds knocking him into another solar system he would not emerge from for another twelve hours. His body lay supine like a corpse, beneath the light bed sheet, and Jennifer realized she had been living in a house of mourning. She stood before their bedroom mirror regarding herself, the first tiny creepings of crow's feet at her eyes. All those years of Bikram yoga, meditation, and healthy eating had left her body lean and supple like a bullwhip. But how many more years could she maintain such control over her body and its whims? Most of her friends had already tumbled down the rabbit hole of time, emerging as unrecognizable translations of their former selves. Victoria Barber had gone slack at the waist and hips after giving birth, her face spattered with an angry birdshot of rosacea. Cody Griffin cropped her hair short and wore it in a salt-and-pepper military cut. One of her silicone breast implants had ruptured, leaving behind a cruel scar and endless bouts of recrimination and depression. Others had simply let themselves go, wearing bright velour pantsuits and fleece vests to the supermarket and beyond, while some had turned ever so gradually into their mothers, right down to the needling tones of their voices.

She was the only person she knew of her cohort who still looked better without her clothes on than she did fully dressed.

Jennifer folded up the Slut List and placed it gently beside her purple vibrator at the back of her underwear drawer, then removed her wedding ring and dropped it into a kitschy Graceland ashtray full of loose change at her bedside. She dressed quickly so as not to give herself the chance to reconsider; she couldn't bear the thought of seeing Chris quaking again in his sleep, so she changed her clothes in the blind dark of the hallway, slipping into a spaghetti strap tank top and tasteful mini skirt, a forbidden thrill racing through her blood.

She rode the subway ten, eleven stops to another neighborhood where she was certain she knew no one, and climbed to the street, her wedge heels tack-tacking on the gray pavement. The trees were in full bloom, and they smelled like fresh sperm. Before long she found a discreet-looking pub called Feckin Eejits. Two pale, unshaven men smoked beneath a lank tricolor Irish flag. They took no notice of her as she entered the bar, busy as they were cursing each other out about something she could not determine.

Jennifer took a seat at the scratchitti-etched bar across from a mirror plastered with old newspaper clippings of Sinn Fein martyrs and a heroic color portrait of Gerry Adams and his virile gray beard. She ordered a Tanqueray and tonic and scanned the quiet room. Anonymous groups of two or three talked quietly around small round tables, sipping dark beer from pint glasses, their turned backs providing the practical effect of body armor. The bartender wore his hair short like a parochial school delinquent, and a pair of round, gold-framed glasses that gave the impression of extreme stupidity; he was clearly overcompensating. A handsome dark-haired man smiled at her from down the bar and raised his glass in greeting. His black hair looked somehow *edible*, slick like licorice candy. His face had character. He smiled again, and she felt a rush of wetness between her thighs. Jennifer popped the lime wedge into her mouth and sucked out the pulp, the man with the edible hair watching with exaggerated amusement. She imagined going back to his place, and him fucking her with hard-driving hip thrusts, then teasing her with the slow withdrawal of his cock, withholding it, withholding it, and then when she could not take it anymore, slamming it home so his balls slapped hard against her ass in an oh-god explosion of electrified nerve endings.

He was walking over to her now, and she felt excitement thrilling through her veins. She had forgotten how easy it was. He moved with the confident swagger of an upwardly mobile six-figure man used to getting what he wants. But when he came around the bar, she saw what he was wearing on his feet, and instantly lost interest. He wore those hideous toe shoes, red ones, that promised to give the benefits of running barefoot without actually being barefoot. They looked ridiculous, like flippers, like clown shoes, like a cold shower, and Jennifer threw the remainder of her drink back in one burning gulp.

"I see you'll be needing another," the man said, a wry smile on his lips.

Jennifer scoured her brain for her travelers' Portuguese, picked up during a semester abroad in Brazil nearly twenty years ago. "*Desculpe, eu não falar Inglês.*"

The baffled expression on his face made her want to laugh out loud, and he tried again, though circumspect this time, lacking the rooster strut of his previous statement. "Do you mind if I buy you a drink?"

Do you mind? Jennifer laughed, flashing her teeth at him and threw at him the cruelest Portuguese she could remember. "*Burro de merda!, Burro do caralho! Toto! Rego do cu! Pichota! Picha!*" And she finished with her favorite, "*Olho do cu*—asshole," which she remembered literally meant, "The ass's eye."

After he had beat his retreat out of the bar, Jennifer heard a slow clap of congratulations at her back. She turned to see a slim long-haired man with a ragged beard sitting alone at a round table applauding over his empty pint glass. He wore large black gauges in his ear lobes and had colorful, intricate tattoos running the length of both arms. His septum was pierced like a cartoon bull.

"Nicely done," he said, rising from his table. "You just cut his balls off and fed them to him for dinner."

At first glance, he was not attractive—skinny, unkempt, and consciously alternative with a capital *a*, a little too downtown for her taste. But, as he approached her, she saw his tattoos in detail, one of which featured a blue-limbed bird-like creature devouring a naked woman whole. Beneath that, the figure of another unclothed woman found herself trapped from the waist up in a translucent blue egg. They were beautiful nightmares, and his black eyes were pure darkness, reflecting nothing. She wanted to search those eyes and find herself in them.

"I'm Magpie," he said, extending his hand. There was dirt under his fingernails, and she recognized the familiar sweet sandalwood smell of Nag Champa on his skin.

"Jane," Jennifer said.

"Sweet Jane," he whistled tunelessly. "Well, now that we know each other, let's get out of here."

It was not a question and she obeyed. In the street, he lit a hand-rolled cigarette and expelled smoke into her face. "Your tits are small," he said. "That's nice."

The sun had set completely now and they walked side-by-side down a quiet tree-lined street. He seemed to have entirely lost interest in her, smoking his cigarette with fascination, blowing double smoke rings perfectly, one inside the other.

She realized she could not place his age, twenties, thirties, older? So she asked him how old he was.

"I'm five hundred and sixty-two years old," he said, stopping short in front of her. "You're in your early forties, right?"

"I'm thirty-nine," Jennifer responded, wishing she'd given a more playful answer.

"Doesn't matter to me."

Magpie's studio was on the top floor of an industrial garage that smelled of motor oil and burnt metal. When he flicked on the overhead light, Jennifer was surprised to see how neat the place was. The apartment was furnished in minimalist style and the polished oak floors were bare and uncluttered. Two framed pieces of art hung on an exposed brick wall over a black leather couch. Magpie pulled an unmade Murphy bed down from the opposite wall and went to fix them both a drink at a marble island separating the living space from the kitchen.

The pictures fascinated Jennifer and she studied them intensely, forgetting herself entirely. In the first, a black-and-white line drawing, a six-breasted maiden with long hair and pale, luminous skin was bent at the waist against a sylvan backdrop nursing a trio of suckling fawns. In the next drawing, a beautiful, lithe, full-haired woman with a long, slim, erect penis and ample pubic bush, walked awkwardly beside a beastly gorilla of a man whose penis was thick and brutish amid its own wild thatch. They followed closely behind a tiny naked man who led the way with an absurdly enormous erect penis of incredible girth, so large that it obscured his view forward.

"That one is Beardsley. Some people think his work is grotesque, but I think it's beautiful."

Jennifer turned around to see that Magpie had undressed and held two drinks in his hand.

"Drink up," he said, offering a half-full jam jar to Jennifer. "Applejack. It's homemade."

She took the drink and it burned on its way down like cheap sinus-burning brandy. Magpie's cock hung limp like a dirty sweatsock against his pale thigh, and he stood expectantly, his lips parted. "Why don't you get me started."

"Are you going to wash that?"

"We're all God's children. Aren't we? "

"Well, I'd like to use the bathroom."

"Over there, behind the curtain," he said, slapping her on the ass as she passed him.

Jennifer studied her face in the bathroom mirror and asked herself, "What the hell am I doing here?" Magpie was repulsive in every possible way, but his confidence was astounding, otherworldly. She felt now that she was here she had to go through with it, not out of obligation, but out of curiosity. What would it be like to fuck a man who finds such horrors beautiful? She wondered briefly whether he expected her to be shaved; it was never her thing, too Alice Liddell for her liking, but she had let it go with Chris being sick and hadn't trimmed herself in a while.

She imagined Chris at home alone in bed, unconscious, and she tried to muster empathy for him, but it had been so long since he had been the person she had fallen in love with, that she only felt resentment and anger. She was too young to be so familiar with terms like glioma, neoplasm, mesencephalon, corticosteroids—she was not a doctor after all, and had never bargained for Chris's regular vomiting and dizziness and loss of coordination. She reasoned that it could hardly be a problem if she were to fuck Magpie on his unmade Murphy bed. After all, it was Chris who had betrayed her and their dream life.

Jennifer checked her face one last time and pulled back the curtain. She was flushed from drink, but Magpie did not notice. He was already on the bed stroking himself quietly with his eyes closed. He must have heard the curtain rings clacking because he called out, "Strip."

She did so quickly, dropping her clothing carelessly to the floor, and slid her lips over his cock, her tongue flicking up and down the tender, smooth skin of his shaft. It tasted of dried sweat and funk, and when she took it whole, it pulsed in her mouth like a living thing, not a part of Magpie, but something separate, a life force all its own.

Soon he pulled away and entered her roughly from behind. He was larger than Chris, and Jennifer could feel her organs shifting at the hard slamming of his cock. She felt like she was being split in two.

Magpie whispered, “I'm going to fuck you so you stay fucked.”

It was not an unpleasant sensation, just different, with Magpie's ammoniac breath huffing humidly at her ear. She focused on his cock sliding in and out of her, aware of her slick, inflamed cunt accepting him like a gift. He slapped her hard on the ass, and her entire field of vision turned red for an instant. Then he was biting her neck and shoulders and back and wrapping her hair in his fist and pulling it taut so that her scalp barked at the pain. She focused on the intake and outtake of her breath, the rhythm of their two bodies moving in sync, like a ship at sea on rough waters.

He came in a sudden rush and moved slowly back and forth inside her for a long time before he pulled out. She climbed on top of him and kissed him on the mouth, and he pulled her close with surprising desperation. His pock-scarred chest was pale and concave, a Latin phrase tattooed across his pectorals in brave Gothic letters. She rode him closely, their sweat-coated torsos sticking and unsticking with their movements. Up close, there was something beautiful, almost hypnotic about his face, those black eyes, still empty and dark and inscrutable even as he was inside her.

Jennifer felt the burning sizzle of lightning bolts gathering at her heels and fingertips, a swirling hurricane of energy surging throughout her body, a rising crest of colors, rising, rising poised to explode. She ran her fingers through his long hair, grasping his scalp with her short nails. Her finger slipped into a hole in his skull, and she froze, terrified, her orgasm stillborn in an instant. Something was deeply wrong with this man, that hole in his head. He was still cupping her ass with his hands, easing her forward when she said, "Stop."

He did so, a dreamy smile on his glowing face.

Jennifer could still feel his cock beating inside her, his blood pumping. She rolled off him and lay beside Magpie on the bed, a queasy feeling in her stomach.

"What is that?" she asked. "That hole."

"The hole in my skull?"

"Yes, that one."

"It increases the flow of blood to the brain and creates a sort of higher consciousness, like being permanently high." He stroked her back, but there was nothing erotic in his touch now. "It's better than mescaline, better than mushrooms."

Jennifer wasn't sure if he was joking, but his unsmiling face told her he wasn't.

"You put a hole in your own skull?"

"It's the oldest surgical practice known to mankind. It's been performed for thousands and thousands of years, all the way back to prehistory."

"And you walk around with a hole in your head."

"Not all the time. I've got a cylinder plug made of polished bone."

The sweat cooled to ice on Jennifer's skin, and she felt revulsion at the grotesque horror show that is the human body beneath the skin. Nothing had ever felt so wrong to

Jennifer before. "What *are* you?" Jennifer said, wrapping his sour bed sheet around her shoulders.

"You know that feeling when you do a headstand? Instead of the blood pumping upward from the heart to the brain, it gives the heart a chance to rest, and washes the brain with oxygen, refreshing the hypothalamus and pituitary glands, the pineal gland, you know, the third eye with fresh blood, nutrients. "

"And I suppose you are some kind of doctor."

"I'm not a 'doctor' doctor, maybe a medicine man, maybe a shaman." Magpie chuckled patronizingly. "Sweet, sweet Jane."

"You know, my name's not Jane."

"Names don't matter. Only the spirit matters. I am Magpie today, but tomorrow I might be Imhotep or Khufu or Hieronymus Hitler." He rolled over and shuffled through a chest of drawers beside the bed. "I've got an idea."

He opened a small velvet-lined wooden box which contained a small drill, a surgical scalpel, hypodermic needle, and several vials of clear liquid. "Are you feeling open-minded?"

"Are you out of your mind?"

"Yeah, yeah I am, and you can be too." Magpie laughed, as if he had made a joke. "Forty-five minutes to enlightenment. It won't hurt. Tetracaine hydrochloride will take care of all your worries. I've got some heavy-duty Canadian antibiotics in the fridge, so risk of infection is low." He caressed her hair almost lovingly as he spoke. "I'll take you places you've never imagined. Just wait till I'm inside you. It won't hurt a bit."

"Wait," she practically screamed, pulling back from his tender caress. "You want to fuck me in the head?"

"I just want to increase the flow of blood to the brain, the sexiest of all sex organs, and then I'll just slowly insert the glans, the head of my penis into the orifice, not deep, just the tip. You will feel like you did when you were fifteen again, like you've been touched by the index finger of God. Intimacy on a cosmic scale."

Jennifer trembled beneath the bed sheet, horrified. "I think I'm going to throw up."

"There's a basket beside the bed."

"I have a husband at home. He is sick in bed with a brain tumor and he's going to die, and you, you just casually talk about drilling a hole into my head."

Magpie looked genuinely shocked. "I didn't know you were married. I don't need that kind of static in my life." He whistled tunelessly again. "I thought you were some desperate cougar in need of a good screw."

"Well, I'm not."

"I'm not judging. The body needs what the body needs."

"I didn't need this," Jennifer said. "I didn't need it at all. You disgust me."

"When was the last time you were fucked, I mean really fucked?"

Jennifer was silent for a beat, "Asshole." And then again, barely audible, "Asshole."

"You'd better get home to your man. He needs you."

Jennifer gathered her clothing off the floor, feeling her throat constrict. "You know, you're a sick fuck."

"Go home, Jane Doe. That's where you belong."

Out in the street, Jennifer looked back once at Magpie's apartment, his studio light still on above the garage. She caught her breath, with a deep shuddering intake, a tide of darkness sweeping over her. *What have I done?*

Jennifer walked in no particular direction, her feet carrying her anywhere but home, deferring the moment in which she would have to face Chris. Of course, he would know immediately what had happened. She looked like she'd been mauled by a werewolf, her skin chewed raw at the shoulders and neck, her hair a sweaty tangle, Magpie's animal scent all over her. She walked, farther and farther from where she was supposed to be, numb, throbbing, streetlights flashing from red to green, her breath shallow, stricken, knowing that a life of regret and remorse awaited at the end of her journey.

MARABOU

The safari went better than planned, and Todd Spicer was anxious to return stateside to show off his prized photographs. He had seen wildebeest, by the thousands, miles and miles of them tramping across the Serengeti, their idiot grunts filling the air as he caught them in his viewfinder. He had snapped gray elephants with their babies, drinking at a murky watering hole, their lazy tails swishing flies out of the air. He had photographed rhinos, giraffes, leopards, and cheetahs in their natural habitats, so different from the sterile zoos back home, that he had laughed out loud at the sublime justice that his severance package was paying for this entire trip. His prized shot featured a marabou stork feasting gruesomely on a dead zebra, its luminous ribs showing through where it had been picked clean.

Todd had jumped out of the Land Rover to gain a better angle, and the Maasai driver, Henry, had shouted for him to return immediately to the vehicle. But his new telephoto lens could not provide the critical point of view. The stork looked like a stern undertaker with its black wings cloaked over its narrow shoulders, its bald, pink head mottled with the zebra's fresh blood.

"Get back in the Rovah! Is bad luck," Henry called.

Todd could hear a rhythmic clacking coming from the stork and edged closer, ignoring Henry and the frantic pleas of his timid companions, who had run from simple field mice scurrying through their camp. The sickly sweet smell of the zebra's flesh was overwhelming in the dry heat, and Todd stifled his gag reflex with comforting thoughts. Its body was peppered with hundreds of roiling flies, visible against its matted white stripes. The stork, with its pale, thin legs, was victory, vengeance, feasting on a beast dozens of times its own size. Todd wanted to possess this hideous creature, make it his own, hang it on his wall as a reminder that the winner is the survivor, and the vanquished forgotten.

The stork turned its head suddenly, and Todd saw its sharp beak in profile for the first time, like two knife blades. It charged at him, spreading its massive wings and knocking him to the ground. Despite his shock, Todd had the presence of mind to snap two or three pictures before Henry grabbed him under the arms and dragged him back to the Land Rover.

When they reached the hotel in Dar es Salaam, Todd begged off invitations to take a ferry to Zanzibar for the day. The city was filthy, with trash and refuse scattered everywhere, and he had no desire to leave the sanctuary of the hotel just to make his way to a crowded ferry boat. Ten days with his fellow travelers on the Serengeti had been enough, and he didn't care if he ever saw them again.

His head ached from too much sun anyway and as he dropped down into the middle of the bed, he felt he could sleep forever. But he could not sleep, and after an hour or two of shivering beneath his sweat-drenched blanket, he gathered enough strength to drag himself across the room to turn off the wheezing air conditioner. He was shuffling back to the bed when he discovered the smooth, raised eminence at his groin, and another beneath his armpits. He fingered the tender swelling, and his eyes filled at the surprising pain.

He found the bedside telephone and called down to the front desk, "I need a doctor."

Todd did not recall having fallen asleep. However, when he opened his eyes, it was nighttime, and a large pulsing moon filled the upper half of his room's tall window. In the darkness he heard the breathless overlaying of voices very close by, spoken in savage, indecipherable Swahili. Strange, distended shadows danced jaggedly against the bare whitewashed wall of his room. In his terror, he tried to recall the words he was seeking, but when he called out, no voice came. Todd raised his cramped fingers to his mouth to discover they had turned black at the tips. Was he turning into one of *them*? His friends at home had joked that he was going to go native, but this was impossible.

A very black man wearing round, wire-rimmed glasses appeared before him, his face crisply officious. "Mistah Spiceah," the man said. "You are very, very sick. You cannot stay here."

Three men wrapped him in a bed sheet and loaded him into a wooden cart, strewn with ragged bits of dry switchgrass. They carried him roughly down the back stairs, bouncing the wheels as it went, each concussion shooting pain into every quarter of his being. The three men stopped on a landing between floors allowing Todd the opportunity to vomit. The men laughed as if someone had told a hilarious joke.

As they wound their way through the nighttime streets, Todd wondered why they had not simply called an ambulance. They moved in a silent procession as Todd trembled uncontrollably, nearly tumbling out of the cart. One of the men took off his shirt, tore it into strips and tied Todd's limbs to the cart's wooden slats.

The moon was a giant, unblinking eye, and Todd climbed into its pulsing center, and saw the world as he had never seen it before, an unbearable truth entering him like a gust of wind.

When the three men arrived at the dump at the edge of the city, the sick man was shivering quietly, a blissful grimace frozen on his face. Nearby, a half-dozen death birds picked their way through a trash heap, beating their black wings in unison to drive off a foraging billy goat. The sick man whispered with some urgency, words the three men could not understand, so they threw him atop a steaming pile of trash and returned to the hotel.

THE PRICE OF ADMISSION

Punk rock Shawn Silver sat on a tree stump smoking a cigarette and swinging his butterfly knife, "What a waste of pussy," he said, his brow furrowed with deep concern.

"What do you mean? I'd still bang her." Hodgson laughed.

Shawn threw a clot of dried mud at him that exploded at his feet, "You wouldn't know what to do if she spread her legs and called you daddy."

We all laughed, including Hodgson, because it was true; he'd never kissed a girl except his cousin, once, when she had had the chickenpox, and redheaded Heenan, though he'd already filled out like a linebacker, was still a crybaby whose eyes glazed over at the slightest insult. I secretly and ashamedly played with Star Wars figures and the original full-sized GI Joes and had only stopped shooting blanks when I whacked off to my French teacher, Madame Liska sometime in the past year. But Shawn had fingered three girls and eaten out a fourth; he told Hodgson it didn't taste too bad because he'd squeezed peppermint toothpaste between her legs and lapped it up like a dog.

It was the day after the Sunshine Girl, Jessie Inwood, was found raped and murdered less than three blocks from our apartment complex. We sat in Forest Grove, beneath the drooping willow tree that had been our de facto clubhouse, base, and meeting spot since Mitchell Levy's millionaire parents had divorced, sold the mansion and pool, and moved away the previous summer. We had come to check out Shawn's stash of Hustler magazines he had stolen from his father the last time he had visited him in Rochester. He had promised that girls did it with girls and with elephant-dicked men who made the most hilarious faces. He even told us that one magazine had a scratch and sniff centerfold while another featured a naked woman smoking a cigarette from her smiling snatch.

"Well, where are they?" Hodgson asked.

"Up there," Shawn said, indicating a towering pine tree near the stream.

"Bullshit," Hodgson said.

"You think I'd leave them out here where anyone can find them? These aren't fucking comic books." He crossed his arms derisively over his safety-pinned Clash T-shirt.

Hodgson looked up through the leaves of the willow, the summer sun sifting down and angling through the trees. "All the way up there? I don't fucking see them." The way his head was tilted, with his iceberg of a nose in the air, he gave the impression he was trying to smell something in the far distance, and Shawn seemed to be enjoying the absurdity of it.

"Higher," Shawn said, laughing. "Right near the top."

"There's nothing up there, you fuck."

"Sure as fuck is."

"Go get them then."

"*You* get them, nutmeat. You scared?" Shawn said blowing out a dented smoke ring. "I'm enjoying my cigarette." He took a pensive drag.

"Heenan, you're the biggest, you get them."

Heenan yawned slowly and said in his flat voice "You're the one that wants them."

"You're scared," Shawn said crushing out his cigarette against the side of his combat boot. "Just admit you're scared to climb a tree."

"I'm not scared of anything shit-smacker," he said standing up so that you could see he had a hard-on pressing against his zipper. He pulled an ivory handled switchblade out of his pocket and flicked open the blade. "Do I look scared?"

"Does the tree?"

"Where did you get that?" Heenan interrupted. "That's cool."

"Head shop downtown."

"My mom gave me my dad's old hunting knife." He yanked an awkward blade out of his belt and held it up for us to see.

"What about you, Kravetz? What do you have?"

I pulled the Swiss Champ pocketknife with thirty-three features I had just gotten for my bar mitzvah out of my shorts pocket. It was as thick and unwieldy as a school stapler and its gleaming cellidor handle shined bright, period red.

"You have a fork and spoon in that thing?" Heenan squinted.

Shawn laughed. "We can all relax now. Kravetz can corkscrew the killer to death, and then file his nails for the journey to hell."

He had always had this way about him, firing the right words at you to make you feel small, idiotic, but somehow you felt lucky he was your friend, because he made things happen. In fact, it was Shawn who had talked his mother into letting him out that sunny, summer morning, despite the fact that a killer was on the loose. She had said as long as he stuck with his friends and carried a knife for protection, it was OK. Most of the Willowdale moms seemed to be divorced and there was sort of a single mother's network that had sprung up, and before you knew it Shawn's mom had called mine and Hodgson's and so on until the four of us were allowed out of our stuffy rooms to enjoy the rest of our thirteenth summer without interruption.

"What are we going to do now?" Hodgson said, spitting at his own feet.

"We can have a circle jerk," Shawn said.

"Very funny," I replied.

"I wonder who found her." Heenan said.

"Found who?" Hodgson responded with annoyance, spitting again at his feet, only this time a long string of saliva remained dangling from his mouth. He batted it away with the flat of his knife.

"Your girlfriend, the cheerleader."

"Aw, she had such great tits."

"They were probably fake," Shawn said. "They all have fake tits, fake hair, fake orgasms."

We could hear cars driving past at the top of the hill and the lazy moan of a 747 further above.

"Free-to-be Steve found her," I said.

"How do you know?"

"I read the paper this morning. There was a picture of him. He was interviewed and everything."

"Lucky guy," Heenan added. "I wish I found her."

"He's got a paper route on her street, and he saw her naked body on the lawn of her neighbor's house."

"For once, I wish I was Free-to-be Steve," Hodgson added.

"That retard!" Shawn said. "I'll bet he's the one who killed her. He's still Damien to me no matter what he calls himself."

We'd all known Free-to-be Steve since third grade, only his name had been Damien, not Steve at all. From the first day he walked into Miss Keane's class, we knew he was different, with his wild unkempt Afro and wide eyes. He ate chicken hearts and liver for lunch and once shit on the floor of the school bathroom. When he lost out on the lottery to take Abercrombie, our class guinea pig, home for the weekend, he poured vinegar in its water, killing it. Most of us had snuck into the movie, *The Omen*, and we called him Satan, wrote 666 on his desk, and punched him in the balls at recess. When my mom talked me into playing with him one day after school, he showed me his shriveled penis and chased me around his living room. He missed the first few weeks of sixth grade, and when he finally arrived, he told the teacher that he wanted to be called Steve now.

"Steve?" Shawn had protested. "He's Damien, or I'm Sid Vicious."

"Now class," Mrs. Walters said, shaking her head in disapproval. "He's free to be Steve, if that's what he wants."

And that's how Damien, son of Satan, became Free-to-be Steve.

"Do you think he fucked her?" Hodgson said.

"What are you talking about?" I said.

"You know, sloppy seconds."

"What do you know about sloppy seconds?" Shawn said, clearing his nose lumberjack style.

"There's no one around, it's still dark. What would you do?"

"Her face was all bashed in," I said.

"So put a bag over her head," Hodgson laughed.

I had seen her at the mall a few times with her mom, and she looked clean and bright, with a straight confident walk like a real adult who had places to go. It said in the paper that she was saving money for college. She was December on the Sunshine Girls calendar, and she wore a sort of Santa bikini and hat, and she straddled a stuffed reindeer like she was riding a pony. But she didn't look like the rest of the girls: salacious April, bent over, lips puckered with a come-hither look on her painted face; July in a wet T-shirt, her nipples announcing themselves proudly through the veneer of cotton; November, hiking a football through her long stockinged legs.

"That's not funny," I said.

"Sounds like Kravetz has a crush on the Sunshine Girl," Hodgson said.

"It could've been your sister."

"Keep my sister out of this," Hodgson said. He spat again, and then shook his head as if banishing an idea from his brain. "You better shut up about my sister."

"Her name was Jessie Inwood."

"Oh, poor you," Hodgson said. "You wanted to fuck her."

"I did not."

"What are you, gay?"

"They're both tall, fair-haired…"

Hodgson was right in my face now. "She was just a stupid slut who was asking for it." He had sour milky breath, and I could see the first signs of a mustache forming on his upper lip. "She was asking for it, all right?"

"I just want you to think," I started to say, before he pushed me down hard on to the rocky forest floor and sat on my chest.

"Don't think, all right?"

Shawn got between us before I had a chance to fight back. "Break it up, girls." He pulled Hodgson off me and ripped my T-shirt in the process. "Go back to your corners before I pile drive the both of you."

I could tell that Hodgson still wanted to get at me by the way he was kicking at the ground and circling his spit pile with his fists in a clench.

"All right," Shawn said lighting up another cigarette and assuming an authoritative tone. "Obviously you ass-pirates are horny. Tell you what. I'll climb the tree and get the magazines if that's what it takes to keep you guys from humping each other."

"Fine," Hodgson said. "Just tell Kravetz to keep his stupid mouth shut."

Shawn stalked off in the direction of the pine tree leaving me alone with the others.

"I'm going to take a piss," Hodgson said turning to Heenan who followed him into the woods. I could hear branches snapping and the sound of their laughter quickly fading away. Shawn sang "Barbed Wire Love," in his high nasal voice and swung onto a lower branch of the pine tree, digging his combat boots into the trunk for leverage.

And in the sudden silence of the forest, I thought of Jessie Inwood and how she was the first person close to my age I had ever known who had died. It had never seemed possible before; death seemed a thing reserved for grandparents, third world orphans, and the terminally unlucky. But she had always been so lucky up until then. It didn't make any sense to me. I wondered what she had been thinking in that moment right before death when she realized that this dream life was over, and there was nothing she could do any more to change that.

Someone was coming down the hill from the roadway above; I could hear the leafy branches swing and snap back into place but could not see who it was yet. I slipped my Swiss Army knife out of my pocket and flipped open one of the large blades with my fingernail. I could see in the reflection on the cold metal blade that I looked scared, no matter how bravely I tried to set my face. My heart beat hard, as the sound of the snapping branches reached midslope. It was too late to hide. I could see his bald head bobbing up and down through the foliage, and then I heard Shawn call out from the tree above. "Oi! Who's there?"

The rustling stopped, and then having lost his footing in the dry earth, the figure slid down the rest of the hill in a cloud of yellowish dust.

"It's Free-to-be Steve," Hodgson laughed.

I hadn't heard them returning from their piss break and was as surprised to hear Hodgson's voice as I was to see Free-to-be Steve standing before us with a pallid, newly shaved head and a bundle of newspapers in his arm.

"Hi," he said, moving toward us. He still had that haunted look in his eyes, only it took on a new meaning now that I knew what he had seen. "Teddy said some guys were down here."

"Yeah, so?" Hodgson said.

"Got a cigarette?" Free-to-be Steve responded.

"Fuck happened to your head?" Hodgson spat.

Shawn scrambled down the tree.

"Didn't like the way I looked in the paper."

"Well now you're ugly *and* bald," Hodgson said.

Free-to-be Steve dropped his pile of papers on the ground and sat on them. He held another paper rolled up in his hand.

Shawn was breathing heavily from his climb and subsequent sprint. He cleared his nose, lit a cigarette, and said in an unusually nasal voice, "Damien the Devil. Heard you've been busy."

"It's Steve," he said flatly. He didn't look at any of us, but beyond, his eyes focusing vaguely in the distance.

"Free-to-be Steve," Heenan added.

"You're the one who killed the girl," Shawn said.

"I found her," Free-to-be Steve said. He had dried clots of blood on his scalp where he had cut himself shaving, the pale skin as incandescent as a light bulb. He was a big doughy kid and without his hair he looked something less than human. "She was dead when I found her."

"How do you know? Are you a doctor? Did you check her pulse, her blood pressure?"

"She was all purple on her back and legs, where the blood had settled."

"Sick," Hodgson said.

"You touch her?" Shawn said. "She had nice titties."

"Got a cigarette?"

"So, did you touch her?"

"Gimme a cigarette," Free-to-be Steve said.

"I'll give you a cigarette if you say you touched her." Shawn blew a cloud of gray smoke toward Free-to-be Steve.

"I touched her," he said softly after a moment.

"Perv," Hodgson laughed. "What did you do? Fuck her?"

"Gimme the cigarette."

Shawn pulled one out of his pack and held it out toward Free-to-be Steve. "Psych! You fucking addict." Shawn pulled the cigarette away.

Free-to-be Steve sat on his papers, expressionless.

"What are you going to do with those papers?" Shawn asked.

"Gimme a cigarette."

"First tell me what you're going to do with those papers."

"Gonna burn them."

"Because you killed her?" Hodgson said.

"Lay off him," I said.

"I don't like the picture," he said, chewing on his lip.

"Did you fuck her before or after you killed her?" Hodgson said.

"I didn't," Free-to-be Steve started to say.

"Leave him alone," I said.

"Do you want to be an accomplice after the fact?" Hodgson said. "Keep it up, and you're guilty too, fuckface."

"Go on," Shawn said.

"Can I have a cigarette?" he said plaintively. Shawn tossed him a cigarette and he caught it, but the rolled-up paper on his lap slipped to the ground and Free-to-be Steve snatched it up with surprising quickness. "A light?"

"Are you going to tell us what it was like to fuck the Sunshine Girl?" Shawn said, holding out the lighter.

Free-to-be Steve took a deep, rattling breath, eyes cast down. When he looked up, I saw that they were raw and red.

"Gimme a light." He leaned into the lighter and Shawn hesitated for a moment, pulling the flame just beyond his reach so he had to stand up from his pile of papers.

"I thought you were going to burn those," Shawn said. "No lighter, no matches?"

"I forgot," Free-to-be Steve said.

"This guy's pathetic," Hodgson said.

Free-to-be Steve slowly turned his eyes, cow-like to Hodgson, and said, "I fucked her. Twice. Once in the mouth, and once in the ass."

"Shit. He's lying," Hodgson said. "And he's afraid of pussy."

"Yeah," Shawn said probing, "Do you want to stay a virgin forever?"

"When I choked her," Free-to-be Steve said quietly, "She pissed herself."

Hodgson started to laugh, but stopped himself, "Holy shit! You're not fucking joking."

I could see a change in Free-to-be Steve's face right then, the muscles slackening in his forehead, jaw, his eyes brighten just a bit, and somehow, I knew he hadn't killed her.

"What about rigor mortis?" I said. "How did you do it with her?"

It seemed that Free-to-be Steve was anticipating that answer, as he quickly said, "It takes about three hours for the body to stiffen."

"Hodgson's stiff already," Heenan laughed.

"Fuck you," Hodgson retorted.

"Go on," Shawn said. "What did you do first, the ass or the mouth?"

"I couldn't put it in her mouth after it had been down there. It's not clean." He took a long drag of the cigarette and rocked back and forth on his pile of newspapers. "You know she spoke to me once?" Free-to-be Steve began, his eyes widening. "She was a nice girl."

"Enough of that shit," Hodgson said. "Did you come in her mouth?"

He paused for a long time until it seemed that he wouldn't say anything at all. "I had to hold her jaw open, her teeth kept getting in the way. And she kept looking at me and I whispered to her, but she wasn't there anymore."

"What did you whisper?" Heenan said, leaning forward, rubbing himself with the heel of his hand.

"I told her I loved her."

"Bullshit. You killed her because you loved her?" Shawn said. "You just wanted to have your way with her."

"No," Free-to-be Steve said, almost in a trance now. "That one time when she spoke to me, she said, 'I like your T-shirt,' and I told her I drew it myself and she touched my shoulder, right here and she said, 'you're really talented.'"

"You're a really talented liar," Hodgson said. "She'd never speak to you."

"She touched my shoulder," Free-to-be Steve said. "She touched my shoulder."

"Get back to the fucking, Romeo," Heenan said.

"What about her ass?" Shawn said.

"The blood had already drained when I found her," he said. "It was all purple and dark."

Free-to-be Steve started to cry, tears streaming down his cheeks, and then long heaving gasps. He threw his head back and wailed up to the canopy of leaves overhead.

"He's a fucking liar," Hodgson said. "He never touched her, never fucked her. It's all lies."

Free-to-be Steve ran his wrist beneath his running nose. "Can I have another cigarette?"

"Fuck you," Shawn said pushing him back. "Lie to us. Get the fuck out of here."

For some reason I thought that if I could just touch him on the shoulder the way Jessie Inwood had, he would realize that he was not alone in the world, that there were people who could understand him, and everything would be all right. I reached toward Free-to-be Steve but he must have thought I was trying to push him away like Shawn had done, and he grabbed my wrist and yanked me into his arms.

It was Shawn who saw the knife first. He must have had it hidden inside the rolled-up newspaper, a foot-long butcher knife, its gleaming steel blade surprisingly cold against my throat.

"You want me to be a killer?" Free-to-be Steve said unsteadily. "Give me a cigarette."

Shawn tossed him the pack and Heenan ran off into the trees screaming and kicking his legs as if chased by a swarm of yellow jackets.

"Pick them up," Free-to-be Steve said. I could feel him breathing hard behind me, his chest heaving against my back, his warm breath at my ear.

"Whoa Damien," Shawn said. "Let him go."

"It's not Damien. All right?" He tightened his forearm across my neck making it difficult to breathe. "Light a cigarette and put it in Stuart's mouth."

Shawn did so, and as I breathed cigarette smoke directly into my lungs for the first time, I realized that my execution was imminent and that I'd be with Jessie Inwood soon, wherever it was that she had gone.

"Let him go," Hodgson said feebly. He fumbled half-heartedly for his knife. He looked pale and scared.

"Drop your knives," Free-to-be Steve said. He gulped out each word separately and then took the cigarette from my mouth and drew on it thoughtfully.

Shawn and Hodgson dropped their knives, but Free-to-be Steve did not immediately let up his grip.

"My name's Steve," he said, loosening his arm a bit, as if there were something deeply soothing to him in that name. "Call me Steve."

"Let him go, Steve," Shawn said without the familiar mocking tone in his voice.

"Let him go," Hodgson echoed.

I felt myself melting back into Free-to-be Steve, his body warm and soft, his heart beating insistently at my back.

"I want you two to kiss," Free-to-be Steve said flatly.

"What?" Hodgson practically screamed.

"Kiss each other. On the lips."

"And then you let him go?" Shawn said.

"I'll let him go."

Shawn grabbed Hodgson's head and brushed his dry lips across his mouth. Hodgson pushed him away, "Fucking gross."

"OK. You'll set him free, Free-to-be?"

The knife had begun to draw blood at my neck, a superficial wound that looked gorier than it was, the blood dripping down onto my T-shirt and shorts.

"Holy shit," Hodgson said.

I could feel Free-to-be Steve's calm breathing behind me; he was slowly finding his equilibrium. "I want you to kiss each other. With tongue. A long, deep kiss, like boyfriend and girlfriend."

Shawn and Hodgson stood silent, their arms at their sides, as they both turned their heads slowly toward each other. Hodgson scratched his pimply chin as if calculating the cost, "Fuck it," he said at last. "I'm no fag."

I could feel the blood dripping down my neck and my voice rose to an embarrassingly high pitch, "It's like giving CPR, or sharing a soda. Just do it already."

Shawn turned casually to Hodgson, sizing him up, "I've made out with girls worse than you."

"One full minute," Free-to-be Steve said. "Then I'll let Stuart go."

"A minute!" Hodgson said. "How about thirty seconds?"

"Call me Steve and its thirty seconds."

It was like a vacuum had come and sucked up all the sound as Shawn tilted his head toward Hodgson's and with the earnestness of a courting lover pressed his lips against Hodgson's open, parted lips.

"Grab his ass," Free-to-be Steve said. "Pull him tight against you."

They looked like two trees that had come together over the centuries and fused as one, Shawn's face above Hodgson's pressing down. Free-to-be Steve loosened his grip on me. I could have broken loose now if I had wanted, but I was transfixed, not only at my two friends making out beneath the forest canopy, but by the change in Free-to-be Steve; he melted and fell against me for support. "I told you I touched her, and I did." I felt his warm tears against my back. "I just, stayed with her, held her hand until the police came." And now he broke into discrete sobs, spewing snot and saliva between his words, "I . . . didn't . . . want . . . her . . . to . . . be . . . alone."

Shawn and Hodgson seemed to be lost in the kiss, their eyes closed, their crotches pressed hot against each other. Thirty seconds had passed by now, but they kept kissing. Steve stepped back, patted me on the shoulder and said, "Sorry Stuart," before he bent and picked up his pile of newspapers. When he was halfway to the hill, Shawn and Hodgson must have sensed it was OK to stop, because they opened their eyes at the same time and immediately jumped back from each other as if they'd been slapped.

"It's Steve," he called back at us. "Just Steve" and he tossed the newspapers high into the air and disappeared beneath the overhanging leaves of the trees. And for one final moment, the shining face of Jessie Inwood smiled back from one hundred cascading newspapers, the Sunshine Girl, floating on the air above Shawn and Hodgson, her smile bright and confident and alive.

"Don't ever tell anyone about this," Hodgson said, pounding his fist into his open palm.

"That's right," Shawn said. "Don't ever fucking tell."

And I never did.

DOG WHISTLE

When he was young, my brother Noah was the most beautiful thing: his long, girlish eyelashes; his pale, pink lips parted like a wound in need of healing; his lean body too fragile for this world.

We were military brats, Irish twins—me born in February, him, just ten months later—but when I looked at him, I saw only myself. With Dad in Kuwait and Mom busy somewhere on base, with Jim Beam and her undiagnosed darkness, we had just the dogs to keep us company, those left behind when their masters went off to war. We would practice our German on Herr Schmidt the bulldog and teach him to beg. Nancy's coat would shine beneath our brushstrokes, and Lucky finally learned to fetch.

Oskar the blind shepherd would curl up beside us in bed, and we'd feel his breathing like a blessing on our young skin. There was always an ache inside me, the need to return to Noah, to be whole again, and we slept with clutched hands, our hearts beating against each other, our breath mingling in the stillness of sleep.

I was thirteen, and he was twelve, and Dad was in Kosovo advising NATO on their bombing campaign. My brother's long black hair had grown to the middle of his back, and nobody could touch it but me. We communicated wordlessly; a look, even a thought, could light me up like a bonfire. We both *knew* at the same moment that

Herr Schmidt had died, and in our grief, Noah fit his body neatly into mine, pressing himself so deep I knew I would never die. "Ich liebe dich," I thought the entire time, "Ich liebe dich." The sweet pain of him pulsing inside me was the most natural thing in the world.

In the woods a few kilometers from base, we found a shaded spot beneath a linden tree and buried Herr Schmidt there. But my brother was distracted and for the first time I didn't know what he needed. A stag had shed its antlers nearby and my brother picked them up, caressed them tenderly, the way he had touched me. I opened my mouth to speak, but no words came.

My brother grew ugly. His shoulders broadened, a smudge of fuzz appeared above his upper lip, he cut his hair short and carried with him the unashamed tang of burgeoning masculinity. My breasts came in small, a pair of dove's wings grounded from flight. He wouldn't look at me while we undressed, but we continued to experiment, tasting each other's salt, filling each other with our needs, but never again did I think "I love you."

He kept the antlers at the head of his mattress, and he would cut himself with their sharp points, awaking with a pulsing star of stigmata on each of his palms, a slash on his wrist.

I knew when I woke alone that winter morning that he was gone for good. He had been hurting himself more and more—whittling away at his skin with the rough edge of the antlers, impaling himself upon them until his skin broke. When I finally found the voice to ask him to stop, Noah placed the antlers on his head, turned his back, and left me alone in our bedroom.

SAUDADE

It's as if she really has died this time, as if those pills you worried so much about finally did their merciful job, washed down with a glass tumbler of white wine, her slim body laid out in perfection on her unmade bed for eternity.

But you know she is still out there, like lightning knifing the horizon, close enough to stir you awake at four in the morning, but far enough that you know you can never touch her. She has disappeared from your world, those offhand texts which assured you were never alone: "I put a sign next to the dead squirrel saying: free squirrel."; "I saw some new gluten-free cookies, and I thought of you."; "Did you ever wonder why Annabel Chong didn't get her teeth fixed?"; "I'm afraid I'm turning into my mother."; "I wish I liked you more."

No goodbye, nothing at all.

You messaged and you messaged and you messaged and finally you typed: "Fuuuuuuuck! Really?" Because what else could you say that wouldn't make you ashamed for caring so much? You removed her number from your phone, but it still auto-fills when you type the letter *D* with this warning in place of her name: *Don't be a schmuck.*

You knew it was coming from the moment you met her, and every time felt like it could be the last. That first flash of panic in the Morgan Library's East Room, hip to hip beneath the majesty of three stories of inlaid walnut bookshelves—rare books, illuminated manuscripts—and a Gutenberg Bible at your backs. And then that empty space at your side, and she was gone. You found her half an hour later in the Rotunda chatting quietly with a security guard about the provenance of the hall's variegated marble columns. You learned quickly she had a habit of leaving rooms without a word, as if preparing her whole life to simply vanish, but you never got used to it.

Walking barefoot through the scrim of water in the courtyard of the National Portrait Gallery, she told you the word "scrim" is being misused: "It's a light, gauzy material, more of a screen, used in theater to create special effects." Then she said, "The next time you visit, we should bring a picnic lunch."

That was the last time you saw her.

Or was it the time you visited Ivy Hill Cemetery in Rosemont, stopping for a moment by the grave of Nathan Hurley, a thirteen-year-old boy who died in a car wreck? She seemed to make a point of walking two or three steps ahead of you the entire time. And then, on the Metro, you remember now, she kissed your neck and left the impression of her sweet red lips that you didn't notice for hours.

She is—it is almost impossible for you to write the word "was"—the smartest woman you have ever known, but you don't need a qualifier; she is the smartest *person* you have ever known, so curious, unpretentious, surprising.

She knows the meaning of the word "weltanschauung," motherfucker, but would never use it in a sentence. One minute she'd be telling you a story she heard while working at the State Department about the capture of

Khalid Sheikh Mohammed—the next, why Sasha Gray is her favorite porn star. You exchanged book recommendations and music recommendations: Roth for du Maurier, Alex Turner for Alabama Shakes, you for her. You made her furious the time you mocked a song she sent you because it was auto-tuned. She said you are not a kind person: "It's not an insult, but a fact, like saying I have brown eyes." Another time she said: "That is the nicest thing anyone has ever done for me."

When she cried to you on the telephone and said she is afraid to die alone, you said you would always be there; she is your favorite person in the world. She told you about the terrible, awful, horrible dates she had been on since she dumped Matt: "This one doesn't read."; "This one was funny in person, but his MGTOW blog was bro-tastically sexist, and I refuse to be a collaborator."; "Why does anyone think emailing a picture of his junk is the least bit appealing?"

You burned when she told you about the time she'd wasted making herself up, applying bite-red lipstick alone before her mirror, black eyeliner, a hint of citrus perfume—bitter like lemon, then slipping on her stockings, stepping into four-inch heels. One night, she FaceTimed you as she unfastened her corset, and you asked her why go to all the trouble for these knuckle draggers who can't punctuate a sentence? She told you she just wanted to find someone to bang it out with for a while: "It doesn't mean anything to us millennials. Like, you don't fall in love with everyone who gives you a massage, do you?"

When she said she needed an adult opinion and asked you how many dates she has to wait to admit she's been institutionalized, you wanted to hold her and tell her you know everything and it's all OK.

You really believed you understood her better than anyone else on the planet. You know you knew too much, and you know that is why she is gone. She told you things she had never told anyone before—and will never tell again.

You want to reach out across five states and the District of Columbia and simply say, "I miss you," but what you feel is much, much more, and you can't, because your words will not be returned, and the silence at the other end means the same to you as a death.

You have written hundreds of thousands of words, and you know there is no word in the English language to describe how you feel. But you do recall a song you once heard by a Cape Verdean singer your wife wanted you to take her to see back when you lived in New York.

Saudade.

It is a Portuguese word, and it is the saddest word in the history of language, especially when you are overcome by it, that empty feeling of nostalgia, loss, and the understanding that she will never, ever return.

You can't talk this pain away. You can't write this pain away. You can't sweat this pain away. You can't drink this pain away. You can't fuck this pain away.

That is *saudade.*

ABOUT THE AUTHOR

Jonathan Papernick was born and raised in Toronto, Canada. He is the author of the acclaimed short story collection *The Ascent of Eli Israel*, *There is No Other*, and the novels *The Book of Stone* and *I Am My Beloveds*. His work has received starred reviews from *Publishers Weekly* and *Library Journal* and has been translated into Spanish and Italian. Papernick has taught fiction writing at Emerson College since 2007 and serves as Senior Writer-in-Residence in the Department of Writing, Literature and Publishing. His story, "In Flagrante Delicto" has been adapted into the short film *The Man with the Third Eye*. He has two sons and lives with his wife in Providence, Rhode Island.

ACKNOWLEDGMENTS

First and foremost I want to thank Lou Aronica from The Story Plant for supporting my work and publishing it and putting it out there into the world. Your support means more to me than you can possibly know.

Thank you to Kim, my lovely wife, for putting up with me and loving me.

Thank you to Eve, from your wuzband; I know I wasn't always easy, and you have always been a great first reader for me. You're never afraid to call bullshit on a bad sentence or icky plot point.

Thank you to Caroline Leavitt, my literary guardian angel who has always been good to me and made the shidduch between me and Lou when I needed it most.

Thank you to Emerson College for giving the opportunity for me to teach fiction writing for more than a decade and a half; thank you for a job I love, that gives me the space to work on my writing.

Thank you to Collin Rousseau for loving my writing so much that you have worked so hard to adapt it for the screen. *The Man with the Third Eye* is insane. I can't wait to see what you do with "The Cinq à Sept Girl."

Thank you for the literary journals who published these stories. Thank you especially to Sara Novic, for publishing a pair of my stories with the late, great, *Blunderbuss Magazine.*

These stories are some of the most personal I've ever written so I want to thank all of my future readers for spending some time with me in these pages from whenever or wherever you come across these stories. I'll never tell what is true, but just know, it's more than I will ever admit.